ACCORDING TO KIT

ACCORDING TO KIT

Eugenie Doyle

FRONT STREET
Honesdale, Pennsylvania

Acknowledgments

Writing is a solitary activity, but only to a point. I have the following people to thank for their company and help during the making of this book:

Stephen Roxburgh, for allowing me to stumble into his clear, honest, brilliant editorial path.

Katya Rice, incisive word wizard, for being the copy editor and reader every writer wants.

My niece Margaret Day and friend Katie Flindall, for sharing with me their experiences as young dancers.

Marion Dane Bauer, writer and mentor, for her generous advice and support.

My friend Ellen David Friedman, for caring about Kit at her least mature stage.

My family, Sam, Nora, Silas, and Caleb, for seeing me through the cancer treatments, which transected the writing of this book—Nora, for reading early drafts with unconditional love; Sam, for embodying the farmer frame of mind: *No matter what, get up early, do what needs to be done.*

I would like to thank the gemlike National Museum of Dance in Saratoga Springs, New York, for its inspirational exhibits, especially on the mothers and fathers of modern dance. And, finally, thank you to the Jerome Robbins Dance Division of the New York Public Library for research assistance.

—E.D.

Library of Congress Cataloging-in-Publication Data

Doyle, Eugenie.
According to Kit / Eugenie Doyle. — 1st ed.
p. cm.
Summary: As fifteen-year-old Kit does chores on her family's Vermont farm,
she puzzles over her mother's apparent unhappiness, complains about
being homeschooled after a minor incident at school, and strives to communicate
just how important dance is to her.
ISBN 978-1-59078-474-7 (hardcover : alk. paper)
[1. Farm life—Vermont—Fiction. 2. Ballet dancing—Fiction. 3. Mothers and
daughters—Fiction. 4. Home schooling—Fiction. 5. Family life—Vermont—Fiction.
6. Vermont—Fiction.] I. Title.
PZ7.D7745Acc 2009
[Fic]—dc22   2009007032

FRONT STREET
An Imprint of Boyds Mills Press, Inc.
815 Church Street
Honesdale, Pennsylvania 18431

To all my dance teachers,
especially Claire Mallardi and Patty Smith,
and to all who keep dancing (and farming) against the odds

"Vous avez droit à deux erreurs."
("You have the right to two mistakes.")
   —Montreal highway sign

"And making a false step—doesn't that come from
not knowing how to dance?"
   —Molière, *Le Bourgeois Gentilhomme*

PART ONE

1

Nothing happened. I clarify for Mom over and over on the ride home: *Nothing happened.* She just shakes her head and tightens her grimy fingers at ten o'clock and two o'clock on the wheel. She refuses to let me exercise my permitted rights and drive.

At home she scrubs my foot even when I say I didn't get cut at all. On our way to the barn for chores she says there will be changes. She and Dad will take things in hand. It's November, almost dark at four p.m., and oppressive. I tell her to chill, that I will not relinquish my life, liberty, and pursuit of happiness to a terrorist state, to a reaction based upon fear.

"Kitty," she says. She always uses the cutesy form that I hate. "Why do you have to make things so complicated?"

"*Mommy*, one's children enrich and complicate things. Didn't you know?"

Later, after my clear but futile explanations to Dad at dinner, Mom gives the longest sigh in the history of motherhood and says, her eyes pinched closed, "That school's no place for learning. Homeschool or go to St. Rose's in Burlington, but you are not going back to Greensbrook. Just choose."

My choice is to leave, slamming the door. I march in the cold—thirty-two *grand battement* steps—to Grampa's trailer. Walyo shuffles across the kitchen floor to greet me. My body charged and my mind revved, I listen to the Family Seer snoring in the bedroom. The sound calms me down. Grampa went to bed early; he missed Mom's fit. How deep he must sleep not to hear fits and not to hear his own snores! How nice to be old and to have peace.

Quite the team we are: he, snoring lonely as a cloud in his bed, and I, alone, fuming on the sofa, the very one where a year and a half ago Grammy Rose waited for death. *I* am now waiting for *E.R.*, having missed *Friends* thanks to chores and late dinner prolonged by my unjust "dessert," Mom's demancipation proclamation. And then that sigh, like life itself, leaking out of her unlipsticked lips.

The TV stays off while I wait, because I hate ads. Walyo's contorted on the floor licking between his legs, his flexible spine like a Slinky. Quick, wet licks against Grampa's underlying drone—ah, the music at Snow Ridge Farm! Add Mom's screeching and whining, and *voilà*, our theme song plays.

To that accompaniment I sort thoughts the way I, Cinderella, sorted the Snow family laundry before washing it in separate loads this morning before school:

Filthylight/filthydark/stinkysockswithbristlesofhay.

Delicate light & leotards.

Ma mère does not separate clothes. She gets grease on my tights. I have to take care of myself, my laundry, my life.

Just then, several thumps and Grampa appears, one gnarly hand holding the doorframe, the other scratching under the collar of his pj shirt. It's the blue flannel Grammy helped me make for him one Christmas.

"Weelll, look what the cat dragged in!"

At that, Walyo finds his feet and wobbles to Grampa, who stops scratching his own neck and starts on Walyo's.

"Mom's nuts. She wants me to go to St. Rose's or homeschool just 'cause of that knife thing. I don't get it."

"Your grammy liked St. Rose's. Thought it was named after her," Grampa says.

"No offense, but that was ages ago, and she lived in Burlington. Mom's overreacting. Nothing horrible happened today."

"Guess she just kinda likes you." He limps back into the bedroom and from the doorway tosses me a pillow, then brings along Grammy's nicest afghan. "You show her what's what," he says, plopping it into my lap. "Stay up here all night. That'll fix her wagon." He ruffles my head like I'm another dog, then heads back to the bedroom with Walyo on his heels. "Night, Rusty."

Rusty. Another obsolete nickname, based prejudiciously on the color of my hair. His own nickname is good: G.W., for George Washington. That's his full name, and he *is* our founding father, born on this farm. But Walyo? His real name was Waldo till I, as a toddler, couldn't pronounce it. My rechristening was so cute they kept it, a permanent reminder of my inarticulate infancy.

I wait awhile for the snoring to resume. Then I switch on the TV and call Lacey.

2

HER VOICE IS RAGGED. SHE COUGHS. "I HEARD YOU GOT hurt. I was gonna call. Amber says police were all over school."

"Not true. Are you still sick?"

"I feel like crap. Don't change the subject."

"Amber wasn't even there," I say. "No one was. Three hundred kids were out. During announcements Mr. Thomas kept calling us 'the survivors.'"

"Funny," Lacey says, but it comes out "fuddy." That cracks me up. I'm desperate to laugh. She wants the play-by-play.

I tell her that except for me only the creeps were healthy. Namely, Ryan Weston. Howdy, Cowgirl, he says to me in Biology. Ms. Wiseman tells the three of us there to do research for our science-fair projects and then goes to have coffee or something. I'm reading about bats, which, you know, I admire for their kinesthetic beauty and bug control.

Annoyingly, Ryan sits next to me at the long table, so close I have to smell his nauseating deodorant. He starts clipping his fingernails, one of which lands on the page I'm trying to read. (Lacey interrupts my telling with a gag or a cough.) I shake the nail to the floor and slide my chair away. Then he goes Hey Red, and starts telling me I'm so hot and I remind him of those Halloween candies. "Get it?" he says. "Red Hot!"

He leans over and starts touching my hair. I sweep it away.

I get up and move to the table where Carter Bennett is sitting, the only other kid in the room. He pretends not to notice a thing; he's studying the amoeba page very hard. No one studies that hard. Then Ryan laughs this crazy cackle. He tosses the nail clipper into the trash basket. "Three!" he yells, stands up, arms in the air. Carter gets up like he's really pissed at Ryan and just wants to study. He reaches into the pocket on his leg, pulls out a knife, a steak knife, and jabs Ryan in the shoulder really fast before dropping it. The knife hits the floor and bounces onto my foot, balancing on the strap of my flip-flops. Carter runs out while Ryan's going, "Jesus, Jesus, what the f---!" He's glaring at *me* and he yells, "Jesus, get someone, bitch! What's he, your f---ing boyfriend?" I'm thinking: I just want to read about bats. Now there's a bloody knife on my foot.

"A lot of blood?" Lacey wants to know.

"I didn't even get cut, but Ryan did, so I went to find Ms. Wiseman and then had to spend hours telling the story to the principal, the police, everyone. Actually, they seemed relieved that our version of school violence was so wimpy. They just called parents. No one acted like it was a big deal. Except," I tell Lacey, "ta-da!—my mother. She goes, 'That school's no place for learning! St. Rose's or homeschool.' Some choice. She wanted St. Rose's, I could tell, but when would I dance if I had to spend two hours a day in a car with her, Saint Cynthia, martyr driver? I told her that prolonged time in a car together would be pointless and contribute sinfully to global warming. But when I mentioned global warming, my dad goes, 'Kit, just choose.' "

Lacey says between sniffs and snorts of phlegm that I was lucky. If the knife had cut me after stabbing Ryan I'd need an AIDS test.

"Thanks," I say, "you sound like my mother."

3

My first day home Mom doesn't have her act together, so homeschool means no school. She says, "I'll make some calls and figure it out." She and Dad are distracted because three heifers were missing when they brought the group in from pasture to breed. Meantime, what am I supposed to do, finish homework for classes I'm not in? All my non-contagious friends are in school, my non-friends too. Lacey, recovered, calls from school and says that Ryan Weston is there acting like a hero, his boo-boo bandaged. Carter was suspended and me exiled; how fair is that? And, to make things worse, it's Monday, a day with no dance class.

I could bed cows, wash milk dishes, or some such, but doing a lot in the barn seems a bad idea given my belief that Mom wants me home to work, not to stay safer, learn better, or any of the other good stuff she claims.

I pull overalls over my pj's, ho hum, do my minimal calf chores, return to the house, eat Life cereal. I then practice pointe for half an hour and stretch in the living room till I'm covered with dog and cat hair and almost as flexible as Walyo and Whisper. I read some Emily D. poems. *I cannot dance upon my toes* ... Ursula recently quoted this to explain that she would stop Monday's pointe classes for a while till she felt less exhausted. She's got some bug too, I guess. Maybe caught it from Lacey.

I'm making chocolate chip oatmeal cookies when M&D come in for lunch. They were out with Grampa in the woods searching for the heifers. I don't want to get involved, on principle. I should be in school.

The late fall day is crisp and windy, but both stoves, wood and cook, make the kitchen cozy. Magical me, I conjure the smell of sugar and chocolate.

After lunch Dad says, "Nice having Cinderella home, but too bad she's got no clothes." I throw a napkin at him, which he snaps back at me before escaping upstairs, smiling like an idiot, to take his usual twenty-minute nap.

Mom says, "Kitty, get dressed," in this really demeaning voice while she rattles dishes around in the sink and sighs. Saint Mama, martyr.

"I would get dressed but you're wearing my hairshirt, Mother." I grab cookies and leave.

I love to run,
I love to skip.
Of all the steps
The leap is best.

I leap the thirty-two steps to Grampa's.

I would sit with him in companionable comfort, but it's dark in the trailer except for the flickering screen lights of "Across the Fence," about chainsaw safety. Spooky. Walyo's on the floor by the sofa sleeping with his muzzle on Grampa's boot; I hate to disturb their peace with lights or gripes, so I hand over the cookies and tell him I'm walking to The Hide. Half wishing, half joking, I say, "Wanna come?"

"Walkin's a lotta work. Take a tractor," Grampa says. "Course I guess you're in the school of hard knocks now, aren't ya?"

I leave him winking at me, chuckling, and nibbling carefully on a cookie. Grammy's were better and I almost apologize. But he'd just wave it off. To him a cookie's a cookie; pajamas count as clothes. He's a prince.

Ordinarily I wouldn't go to The Hide, a guy place my neighbor, Clay, built way up in the woods where his land abuts ours. The one time Lacey and I hiked up there soon after it was finished and was being housewarmed with a party we weren't invited to but knew about, she sniffed and said, "Smells like *boy.*" True. Old socks and farts, cigar smoke, and other weird aromas. We hung right by the windowless window about two seconds till Clay saw me and suggested we might want to leave. Lacey said, "We might." Clay is tall enough that he blocked most of the action, which seemed to be boys standing around holding bottles. We left.

Clay's a senior, our hired man since last summer, our neighbor since forever. In a weird way, I know him but I don't.

Anyway, on this my first self-school day, the sky is so blue that colors bounce off the leaves into my eyes. The air is like a kiss. I wish. Warm, tinged in the soft yellow, bright orange, and red of leaves. Sunlight simmers vivid but gentle. A pale moon swells full. Two heavenly bodies visible at once. Sensual, sensational. I ponder writing a poem, but, alas, I have no paper.

I look at the ground. There's no trail except tire tracks where Dad drives the tractor and cart to haul firewood. Like a deer I follow the path; it takes no effort at all to climb the hill and wind along the logging trail into the woods all the way to the cabin on the other side of the old barbed wire that separates our land from the Carpenters'. That's just Clay, his little brother, and his mother now. His father died of lung cancer about the time Grammy died of pancreas cancer. In addition to a rusty fence and chores in our barn we have deaths in common. At least he has a brother. Two kids and one parent might be preferable to one kid and two parents. Might be.

I step high *développé* over the fence and circle the cabin to make sure it's empty. No coons or foxes or porcupines, witches, or boys about. The door has a latch, no lock, and creaks open to a single, dank room still smelling of boy. I envy Clay his special place, even if he does seem to share it with morons, judging from the leftover cig butts, jerky wrappers, and empty bottles from Boy Hunters' First Weekend of Deer Season. I want my own Hide, a dance studio, only better-smelling and cleaner.

There's no space to stretch or dance in the cabin without sweeping first, and even if there were a broom I wouldn't mess with their private stuff. I just sit on a milk crate by the window and vegetate. I unwrap a dusty piece of gum I find in my pocket.

Really, I don't miss the atmosphere of school itself. It's

always about three hundred degrees inside the building and the air is bad. You're always breathing in the air someone else breathed out. Lucky me to have had most classes in the *inner sanctum*, the windowless rooms at the overheated core of the building so named by my Latin teacher. Grammy told me to study the dead language so I'd understand the names of herbs and animals and the Latin Mass if they ever bring it back. The class was fine, the venue crappy.

Now that I think of it, I liked my other classes too. And I wasn't done yet with school projects, the bat report for instance. I like to finish things.

I want to stay away late, past choretime. Just let Mom wonder where I am. Fix her wagon. But this smelly shack is not the answer, not my place. I'll need a better overall plan than this. I wander back the long way, glimpsing Clay's house across the fence. I could go visit his mother, but she's actually sweet and I'm not feeling friendly. I get halfway home, do a bogus balance-beam routine on a fallen maple, then sit, chewing.

The crack and swish of branches makes me jump. I turn around and see nothing but brush and shadows. Must have been a deer, or maybe one of the missing heifers. If I were nice I'd hunt around some. But I don't.

After dark, at the table, Mom says, "Where were you?"

"Walking," I say.

"You missed chores," Mom says at the same time Dad asks, "See any sign of those heifers?"

"Duh," I say to her, "I know." I turn to Dad. "Nope, no sign."

"Kitty, why are you mad? This isn't a punishment," Mom says.

"Oh, really?"

"No, it will be good. Family together, more time for you to do the things you like."

"I like school. I like my friends."

"You said you didn't! You've been saying how boring it is. Your friends can come here." She stops and then starts up again. "Look at it this way. We'll trade you, Kitty, Kit— homeschool for three dance classes a week! Not once or twice like now. A teacher you like and we like. We'll make sure you get there. You can use the college library as long as I'm cleaning there. You can help clean or not. At home you can help and we'll pay you. A farm is a way of life. High school sometimes distracts. It's not just the knife, it's that other boy, what's his name? Ryan. Bothering you. Why spend time with foolish boys? That can lead to trouble."

Wow. A speech. I can only stare at her.

While Mom was stating her case, Dad and Grampa were quiet, eating. Maybe Dad lets her rant 'cause she's five years older. She, at forty-something, is not what you'd call an elegant-looking woman. Her hair is completely white, as if washed by ghosts. But that is another story.

Dad stirs coffee, looking into his cup. "There's stuff to learn here," he says.

In your cup? I'm thinking. But more than arguing, I

want more dance. "Okay, okay. Let's do it. But three classes a week, you promised."

Dad stands up, touches my head. "All right. I'll do the dishes later. I want to fix that chain on the spreader." He grabs his hat from the hook by the door and leaves.

Grampa rubs his chin with one hand, working his thumb against a crusty patch on his pointer finger with the other. He winks at me. "Guess I better give him a hand. Thanks for supper, Cyndy. Come on, Walyo, you old bag o' bones." And up they go and away.

Mom is completely unreal. Friends come here? Not even relatives want to hang around. For instance, Dad, Grampa, and also Grammy and some other dears departed ...

The door opens. Walyo waddles back in, toenails clicking, and lies down, winded. "Guess what?" Grampa, all excited, calls from the entrance. "Them heifers just wandered in, right into the barn! Leave 'em alone and they'll come home, wagging their tails behind 'em. Rusty, come help me tie 'em up."

"Please don't call me that," I say. But I go.

4

After that first day a routine began. We Snows love a routine. Mom finally got lesson plans from the state, or somewhere. Maybe from the homeschooling Donnellys at church. Maybe from Ms. Wiseman at school, who has offered to help, feeling guilty, I bet, for leaving me alone with those two dimwits in science class. Mom's approach to teaching is surprisingly hands off. Workbooks mostly, and activities meant to teach: pay the bills, balance the checkbook with her and make entries in the yellow Farm Record Book, read books from a list, cook and call it Chemistry, make an egg basket, work on my sewing and call it Math and Art both, help vaccinate calves and fill out my 4-H dairy project record book and call it Science.

A full plate indeed. I go to the barn, I go to my room, I go to the woods, I putter in the kitchen. I dance every other day. That's heaven. Mom calls it Phys Ed.

Dad has me splitting and stacking wood, registering calves, and driving the tractor. Really just chores, like before, only more. But he does pay me. We call it a deal.

I begin to get a few ideas of my own for projects: French, for example, or the ballet words anyway. I know quite a few, *beaucoup*, and I borrow books from the college to help with the rest. And bats, *bien sûr*, I don't know why, but they speak to me.

Grampa wants me to study the Bible with him and

Roberta, a nice Jehovah's Witness lady who rescued him from loneliness after Grammy died. He says Catholics don't know enough about the Good Book. Most of the Bible quotes he tosses around come from the front page of *Country Folks*, the paper I use to light the stove. I don't confront him on this. But I decline his invitation.

Not that I am against religion. *Religio, religionis*: sense of right, reverence, awe. Nothing wrong with that. Actually I was very into God stuff till Grammy died. She taught me this prayer to say every morning: *Good morning sweet Jesus my savior, Good morning sweet Mary my mother, I give you my heart, my soul, and my life. Keep me from sin this day and forever.* I said it with her when I was little and then I got in the habit of saying it every day when I woke up. It's even a triplet you can dance to. But I lost my taste for it when she died. Grammy cared more about religion than I ever did. I was just keeping her company, giving my heart to sweet Grammy. I think for me God has morphed into Dance, because only in class do I feel Supreme, Beyond, Divine.

Besides, here's the religion problem in a nutshell for me: there's no commandment, "Honor thy children." I mean, here I am, cooped up at home supposedly for schooling, and my mother just goes about her life, leaving me teacherless to fill the time between dance classes.

And soon enough the worst thing possible happens.

5

OUR ROAD, JACKRABBIT ROAD, IS RUTTED OLD DIRT, SO as I lurch up the hill from dance class toward home, each bump rams into my tailbone no matter where I steer.

"Watch it, Kitty!" Mom grabs my sleeve as the truck hits a particularly big crater. "My back!"

Her back. My life is ending and her back hurts. First the homeschool sham, and now Ursula, beloved blessed beautiful Ursula, brilliant dance teacher, my only remaining teacher, just told the class she's really sick, not just Lacey's cold-type sick. Multiple sclerosis. She's had it for years, but it was in remission, and now it's worse than ever. She said she's not alone. Vermont has a lot of people with MS, mostly women. Her hands went numb when she was sewing costumes for *Carmina* last spring. Her calves go numb while she's shaving her legs.

This grew embarrassing. I stood at the barre hearing all this, trying not to stare at her long legs under her shadowy skirt. To distract myself I thought of shaving *my* calf, that is, clipping my little Jersey, E.D. 7, for the fair. But I couldn't remove Ursula's numb and hairless legs from my mind.

She was still explaining: fatigue, double vision, a ringing in her ears so loud she needs to play music or be in a noisy place to cover the sound. She said she's taken to eating in the college dining hall instead of at home, for the noise! But the worst thing is overheating. She laughed then and slipped off the thin black sweater she always wears. The worst thing, I thought, is seeing you reduced to this undignified recital of symptoms.

Honestly? I had noticed that off/on sweater move during class, but Lacey had told me it was hot flashes from menopause. Sometimes Lacey is so full of it. She thinks she's got the answer for everything. Today she and the college kids all hugged Ursula after her announcement and looked majorly compassionate, murmuring comfort and offers of help. I didn't know what to do. I'll die without dancing.

"Kitty, slow down," Mom says. "Please."

"It is a disaster." I try to explain slowly and clearly this time. "Ursula cannot teach."

"They'll get a sub till she's better." Mom is gripping the door handle like she always does when I drive.

"A sub? Are there dance teachers growing on trees around here? Mom, do you even understand what MS is? Have you been listening?"

"Kitty, don't talk to me like that. I was listening."

"What does MS stand for, then?"

"You're being rude."

My mother is unable to have a simple conversation. As I turn into our driveway, she yells, "Shush. Stop!" She's leaning way forward, changing the subject. "What's that?"

I stomp on the brake. Mom stares, riveted, at the swath of gravel spotlit by the headlights. I can barely make out a shape just beyond the beams.

Mom flies outside and hovers over the dark patch,

takes a few steps further into the shadows. Then I hear, "No. God." She returns to the light holding dead Homer, one of her beloved Silkies, by his yellow legs, a small thing, wispy as dandelion fluff.

"There's more," she says grimly, placing him in the back of the truck. "You can go on to the house. I've got to pick them up."

Of course I don't walk to the house; of course I help. There are eleven chicken corpses and, when Mom does a head count of survivors in the coop, another ten missing. Only a few bodies show bloody wounds or damaged wings. A fox raid, Mom is certain. We've all seen a fox loping regularly along the edge of the sugar woods. Our resident poultry expert, Grampa G.W., says most of the birds probably died of fright. Chickens do that.

Of course I offer to cook dinner, and from the kitchen window I watch the bad, sad business of my parents side by side digging a mass grave in the corn stubble where the dirt is mushy from rain. Grampa rests at the table from a day of chores and rubs Walyo's head. He grumbles, "Older'n Moses, you're a sorry, no-good watchdog." Grampa is not only our fowl and biblical scholar but also our canine expert.

Of course I sympathize at dinner as Mom presents her fox hypothesis *ad nauseam* while we are trying to eat. Once again, Mom takes up all available space for bad news. If she has a problem, no others exist.

6

THE DAY AFTER THE FOX ATTACK I'M RECRUITED TO HELP tighten up the chicken coop. Mom and I spend an hour straightening the wire fence, closing up the holes at ground level, and draping netting over the top of the pen to keep the birds from flying out and hawks from flying in. Mom, somber and sour-faced, moves quickly and forces me to hurry. She says all creatures—coons, weasels, owls, hawks, coyotes, and dogs, not to mention foxes—are poultry predators. As usual, she is excessive. Chickens are so stupid they seem to invite destruction. Take poor Marge, incessantly pacing the perimeter of the fence trying to push her way under. I bet she gets out before long. Looking for Homer, I suppose, but all she'll find is fox teeth. I don't really like chickens. Cows are smarter and smell better.

After lunch I try to read, but God has turned the lights down. It's late November. *Homeschool Health*, one of the workbooks Mom dropped in my lap, contains a list of diseases to study. A long list. We must have a sick world. *Pick one and research*, it says. I'm studying S.A.D., Seasonal Affective Disorder. These are the symptoms: desire to sleep, carb cravings, irritability, difficulty concentrating, being blue. I'm struck by how this describes *ma mère*. She sits wearily by the window shelling dry beans. She eats the cookies I make. She cries over spilt milk, literally. I left the cap off the bulk tank this morning for the first half of milking, and she yelled and looked like she was about to cry. Her eyes are always squinty. She never smiles, never smiles. Not new, but seems worse these days. It really could be S.A.D., or maybe it's just M.E.A.N. (Mom's Everyday Annoying Neurosis). I'll add that to the list of diseases.

At three, Naheema, the best of the college dancers, calls to say there's a meeting at the studio to plan classes till the college finds a replacement for Ursula. All right! I tell Mom and say I'm ready to go. Mom says oh no, we have to milk early—a co-op dinner. She has to bake cake, sorry. She thought I told her there was no dance, that Ursula was sick.

"Are you kidding?" I say. "They are planning what to do; I have to be there. My one chance to do something. Our deal was homeschool but dance whenever. Besides," I say, "don't you have to clean, you know, do your job?"

"Okayokayokayokay." She grabs her bag. Screams, "Let's go!" I say I can drive. She screams, "No! That takes too long!"

It's scary to drive with a madwoman, S.A.D. or no. But we both have to go. She's got work to do, and I've got my passion to practice.

Labor improves her disposition. On the way home she lets me drive. In the kitchen she pulls an applesauce cake from the freezer, saying, "Good enough for who it's for."

I help Clay finish milking while she and Dad and Grampa go to the dinner. I short the heifers and the dry cows on hay after Clay leaves for basketball. I'm too tired to lug any more. Does them good to totally clean their plate every so often.

I too feel better. At the meeting, Ursula, looking pale and tired, told us that the seniors will take turns teaching until the end of the term, not just ballet but whatever they want. At least there will be classes. They need the extra credit, she said with a small smile. I think that was a joke. Next semester two teachers will take over, a couple, former members of some ballet company in Florida. They just had a baby and are looking for a gentler job. Ursula said to me after, "I think you will like Luis and Clara; I picked them with you in mind. Make sure you practice every day. Do your pointe shoes still fit?"

But she seemed to have sadness on her mind. As I left, she was standing on the threshold of her office with her music professor friend, his arm braced on the doorframe above them, his head bent toward hers. She clutched her sweater at the neckline. I heard her whisper something like, "Heartache all the time."

But not in class, I think. She never looked weak or achy when she demonstrated. She teaches ballet, she used to say, because modern dance, her first love, is ironically old-fashioned now, like her—too gutsy for our feeble world. *The world has become numb and afraid to feel. Ballet at least has a stereotype people can buy, an underlying technique so old and solid and hard it can be done as exercise; it can be done as imitation of childhood dream. It sells. Look at kids' catalogues and books: ballerina this, ballerina that, and for kids who will never learn to plié. Very few of you students realize you can learn to feel. Dance is subversive. You can change the world here. At this moment you can be peace, be love.*

But shh, Ursula would add. *Don't tell anyone, or they will shut us down. Just do fondu tenderly.*

Honestly? I guess I had sensed a change in her since September. Not only that every class was different, which it was, as though she wanted to show us everything while she still could, but that there had been a change in how much she cared about making *us* care. She was still talking about feeling, but often this fall she merely presented the combinations rather than forcing us to do them with her voice, her demonstrations. I felt wobbly, like I was waiting for help to arrive. I remember a time I milked all by myself. Mom and Dad had gone to an auction, and I figured I'd just start. Then they were really late but I kept going, skipping the hard cows, taking other shortcuts, figuring they'd fix things when they got back. For two hours I worked alone, panicky, till everything was done but the cows I'd skipped. I began to cry; I didn't *want* to do it all by myself, I couldn't. I was crying when Mom and Dad got to the barn all amazed at how great I'd done. Now, of course, I could do it again, even the hyper cows. But I still don't want to.

With dance I feel the same panic when Ursula doesn't help as much. *With* her it's easy and fun; *without* her it's still fun, but so much harder.

She says: *Open the body like a book. From the spine. See, feel all that new knowledge? Inside out. Open and lift. A spiral out and up. If you want to shut your book, stay home.*

I feel exactly what she means. It is exhilarating. I am open. I am centered. A perfect pillar, no, a spiral of power.

She says we can learn everything in the world through dance, but she can't *teach* us everything. A lot we must figure out for ourselves.

Just as she stopped teaching pointe, she stopped giving a lot of corrections. I miss her hands on my hip, my shoulder. I sort of felt her letting go. I often brought her food from the farm: raw milk, eggs, homegrown squash and onions for soup. Apparently, like with Grammy, good food was not enough.

Before we leave the little changing room next to the studio Lacey and I compare our faces, our legs, our day's schedules. She wants mine; I want hers—not her bod, but parts of her life, including the Subaru just waiting for her to turn sixteen. Also her classes: English, French, Biology, U.S. History, Film Studies. With teachers and other kids laughing and messing around. Also she's in the jazz band, plays clarinet; and she runs cross-country on the days she's not dancing. She has butt-long blond hair, her skin gets a little bumpy but not bad. She thinks she's fat but she isn't, and she gripes about her parents, but they seem okay except, I guess, to each other. Her father, the one who moved out, bought her the Subaru. She made a bumper sticker: *If it's not one thing it's your mother*. But I don't get why she complains. She and her mother shop, even do yoga together, like friends. Her parents take her places. She has everything. Only her legs are a little short and bowed. Also, she's slightly spastic, not smooth. I'm thinking we are friends.

Lacey agrees maybe Mom's problem is M.E.A.N. Or it

could be S.A.D. She says it's a real deal. Her aunt in Maine gets it every winter from not enough sun. She sleeps too much, eats *beaucoup* bread and sweets, loses her sex drive, can't concentrate. Hey, Mom, I don't know about the sex department, but otherwise, if the shoe fits ...

Lacey says they treat it with bright lights, so much per day. All I can think of is how we put lights on a timer in the chicken coop to give them fourteen hours of light or they'll quit laying. Omigod—just another thing Mom and those clucks have in common. Bright light or bust. Bright light or S.A.D. I don't get it. Aren't children supposed to be the light of their parents' lives? Or God? *I am the Light and the Truth*, etc. I'll have to consult Grampa. Could Mom need more wattage than kids or God can provide?

As we leave Foreman Hall I breathe in the disinfectant my mother slopped on the floor and think, *I love this place.*

I don't remember being born, but I do remember my first dance class in this building, which might as well be the same thing. For as long as I can remember, White as Snow, Mom's business, has cleaned here Monday, Wednesday, Saturday, and other fill-in slots. I wonder sometimes if the Hope Springs administration knows Mom learned to clean in a barn. Grampa calls her the White Tornado. Bathrooms in two big dorms and all the common areas in some of the little houses. I used to love going with her on Saturdays and helping. I had my own bucket and rags and my own rubber gloves. Wowie! Hard to believe this was a big deal, but it was. For this reason: we were good. Together we could transform those germ gardens of soap scum and pubic hair into glistening, sweet-smelling tile and linoleum where nothing could grow. We swept, vacuumed living areas and stairs, mopped hallways. We distributed toilet paper and filled soap dispensers.

We cleaned around the kids' stuff, herbal everything, Extreme and Fresh Scent. We said hi to the few students we saw. Most students were still asleep, I guess, or in classes. Four-hour swabbing shifts and in return Mom got money (from which she paid me a pittance if I helped), plus we got to audit classes and use the library and the pool—not that we ever had much time to use them. For Mom, it meant she got to take accounting so she could put the farm records in order; for me, *I got to dance.* That's how it started. Thanks to Mom, Snowy, the White Tornado, when I was nine the world began.

For some reason that Saturday morning we were cleaning Foreman Hall, a classroom building, rather than one of the residences. Empty and quiet, the building wasn't cozy and familiar like the houses we usually cleaned, and I remember I didn't feel like working. I asked for change for the candy machine. Mom said no. Next time, I told her, I'd stay home and watch cartoons or The Science Guy with Grammy and Grampa, or go to the barn with Dad.

I was walking up and down the first-floor hallway with a rag, hitting the walls, trying to snap the cloth against the glass windows of classroom doors the way Dad snapped dishtowels at me and Mom in the kitchen. I heard faint music, plinky and pretty, coming from upstairs. Up I went. The music stopped and I heard a voice, so big, so serious, saying, "No, no, no—this is not dancing, this is knee bends!" A door at the end of the hallway slanted open. I walked to it and stood to the side, peeking in. Fluorescent bulbs made the room brighter than the dreary hallway I'd been cruising. A row of big girls in leotards and tights and pink slippers stood very straight in a line across the back wall, in silence, looking in the direction of the Voice.

The music started again. The girls turned to face the windows at the end of the room. Each girl held on to a wooden railing with one hand and lifted the other, light as air, in front of her chest and gazed into her palm before floating her arm like a wing to the side. The girls made shapes with their legs—diamonds, arrows, long willow spears.

They all looked beautiful, even the chubby one and the one with a long, jagged scar on her shoulder. I remember, honest to God, thinking they looked a little like a string of our cows when we're milking and they're all eating grain. All busy, content, alive. And in our barn we have music too. The cows' tails twitch to it sometimes, they toss a head to it, they lift a foot to scratch. Kind of like a dance. When no one is there, they rest, poop, chew their cud, have a calf or two, slurp into the water bowls, stand up, lie down—at ease, troops! But at choretime, in they come, General Mom and Dad, and they organize those girls, they direct them into eating, putting out milk, looking lively, productive, rhythmic, and beautiful.

Oh jeez, I am not saying that the first dance class that I sneaked a peek at looked like a barnful of cows. Of course it didn't really, and the room smelled partly like rose soap (and not the vapid kind we stocked in the bathroom dispensers) and partly like the dusting spray on my rag and certainly not like *manure*.

But it also smelled of sweat and work and drew me in the way the barn does sometimes. I heard the teacher before I saw her. The Voice strong but sweet as a song. She was counting *One-two-three-four-five-six,* and she came into view between me and the dancing girls. She moved one arm and one leg as she watched them. I watched her long back, her arms conducting, her wandlike legs pointing, swishing the black ripples of her skirt, and it seemed exactly right: what her body showed, and what the music said. I wanted to try what the girls were doing, the whole row together. I wanted to do what the music said.

I must have moved, maybe even taken a breath. The door creaked, and I jerked out of the dream and dropped the dusting cloth. The music played along, the girls kept moving. The teacher turned and saw me as I bent to grab the rag. I ran down the hall to the stairway. I heard the creaky door shut softly.

Later that morning, as Mom and I were leaving the building, a lady held the door for me and for Mom, whose hands gripped trash bags for the Dumpster. I held my duster and ate from a bag of chips Mom had finally caved in to buying for me.

"Are you the girl who was watching the dancers?" the Voice asked.

I looked up. The teacher? I didn't recognize this lady in a black hat and long coat. Only wisps of dark hair escaped the hat and twirled. But how many girls could there have been watching? So I said, "Yes."

"Do you dance?" she asked. I shook my head.

"You do too, Kitty," Mom said, "all over the house, all over the barn. She's always hopping around."

The teacher introduced herself as Ursula Morrissey; Mom said our names. They worked things out. I could take the beginning ballet class every Saturday at nine o'clock while Mom cleaned. "Those kids you saw may be in college, but they're just beginners," Ursula said. I must have looked doubtful because she explained that there was a children's class, creative movement, but "those kids are just babies. You are the perfect age to begin ballet."

Maybe to Mom I looked scared, or maybe she was already throwing up random roadblocks, because she said, "I don't know about every week. Sometimes she might want to stay in the barn with her dad."

But Ursula knew. "Well, come in next week and watch the whole class. See what you think," she said.

The next Saturday I went in before the music started and sat on the floor in front of a huge mirror and watched for the whole one and a half hours. By the end my butt hurt and my legs were asleep because I'd hardly moved. I watched Ursula to memorize what she did so I could try it later. There were about twelve people taking the class: all big girls and one boy, Charles, very serious and very bouncy when he jumped.

From the loose coil at the back of her neck, along her straight back, to her soft-looking black slippers, Ursula seemed magical, a queen. I was smitten. No more Cinderella—I wanted to be royalty.

"Would you like to take the class?" she asked afterward. Mom was peeking in at the door, motioning that it was time to go. When I looked at Mom, she opened her hand to me as if to say it would be okay but didn't matter much to her. I nodded to Ursula and thought, *Yes, yes!*

And then Mom made getting tights, shoes, and a leotard into such a big frigging deal that by the time the next Saturday rolled around, I was sick to my stomach and began my brilliant career hanging around in the barn with Dad.

But I haven't missed many classes since.

There is nothing like it
dance
is feed unlike bread or milk or cheese
dance is more water
filling empty spaces
filling in
carving muscles
carving space
bending time into
a platform, a ladder, a slide

a body wraps around
and stretches
illustrates
creates
dance is vital blood
it is
what
gives
me
life.

After dinner I write that, tack it on my wall, and call it poetry.

When, after telling me about the new teachers, Ursula said to practice every day, I understood. Like everyone living with cows, I know the meaning of every day. My first show calf was called Every Day, E.D. for short, and this year's is E.D. 7. Every day means there's a biological necessity for doing chores on a regular basis. Seven days a week, three hundred sixty-five days a year. It means no holidays, no vacation. It means a routine so close to breathing you might call it religion. Every day means life as we live it. Chores means maintenance, eating and cleaning. Just as we have to eat every day, so does an animal. Our cows can't gather their own, not in winter, and if we set them "free" they'd starve or coyotes would eat them. That's why Dad was worried about those heifers.

I'm glad I know all this, but it still sucks sometimes. Even Dad thinks so, which may be why he's talking about getting a robotic milking machine. Mom, I think, without relentless routine, would be a lost soul. Come to think of it, she's kind of like a robotic milking and cleaning machine, only with a bad back.

7

HER BACK, HOWEVER, DOES NOT KEEP HER FROM SNOOPING
around my room and finding false evidence to reinforce my
incarceration. I might have settled into mature acceptance of
my homeschool status if she hadn't found a way to rub it in.

Early in the afternoon before chores I am trying on
my pointe shoes to prepare for the promised new teachers,
taking the time to urge my feet into tights, ease them up
my legs. I kneel on one knee and reverently slide toes into
the satin box. I cross the ribbons on the throat of my ankle,
then behind; I tie a knot in the hidden hollow behind my
inside anklebone. At first I think they fit.

Whisper bats at the ribbons. "Just watch or go to sleep!"
I say, scooping him onto my bed. I put on the other shoe.

My feet look like foreign dignitaries, elegant but stiff. I
plié in parallel and straighten tall. I push through the arch
of my right foot to the point. It feels hard. *Liquid*, I think
to myself. I do the other foot and press up to the point.
The shoes kill. I sit and redo the whole thing after winding
lambswool around my toes.

Whisper's off the bed, crouching while I retie the ribbons, tail flapping, eyes watching; he pounces and grabs the
tip of a ribbon—his prize. I detach his claws and put him out
and close my door. I stand flat in first position. I can't flatten
my feet inside the shoes, and a cramp begins in the right
where the pole of the hay wagon hit me a month ago. I walk

around my room and try to lift my heart and my weight away from the pain in my feet; I can't. They don't fit.

I have to find the right moment to ask for new shoes.

During chores my feet slide around in barn boots, protected even when I misstep and trip over a hose. Dad runs the gutter cleaner while I milk. Clay is feeding hay-lage. I wish he would do it before milking; then the cows wouldn't dance around so much, knocking milkers off, wedging me between Dora's hip and the stall divider as they reach toward the feed. Dora steps on my foot, but I react so quickly, jabbing her, that she eases off. My feet, my precious feet! If I had boots with pointe shoe boxes I could practice out here *and* protect my toes. After milking I draw a pair on the chalkboard where we write the names of treated cows and cows about to freshen. I picture a black rubber boot, slim, tapering to a box toe. The sole is flat, waterproof, and gently striated to prevent slipping.

Imagine a place where such footwear makes sense. My life! I go to the loft to throw down the night's hay. The loft is full now, in November, and I have to tug on twine so I can pry bales away from the huge pile. When this pile is consumed by daily chewing, in late spring, there will be a wooden floor, a dusty but lofty dance studio. My haven, my buried treasure, my yearly expectation and delight, like Grammy's crocuses and tulips.

You might think my folks would boss me more. Lacey wonders. Said yesterday that she'd run away before she'd spend all day at home. I tell Dad this during milking. Dad says if I ran away he'd come get me 'cause I am his honey. Rhymes with bunny. Dad has read only a few books and only to me. He asks do I want to go back to school. I say I don't know. He says when I do, let him know, and till then I should drop down hay.

Up in the mow there's two black cats waking up. Cy, Smoky Joe? I don't know. Dad names all the barn cats after Red Sox. I stretch my back the way they do. They run away. I *développé* a leg high *à la seconde*. I pull at the bales and roll them down the opening.

Mom's face appears at that spot amid the cloud of chaff. "See?" she says, holding the sad remnants of a squashed joint gingerly between two fingers. "You got nothing good from that school. You didn't used to do what everyone does!"

She *says* she found it on my floor when she was "cleaning." But that's a lie. It was in my dresser drawer. I say it isn't mine, which it isn't. I got it from Clay's friend Mike when he had it lit in the barn. He passed it to me and I sort of panicked and stamped it out. He's so dumb. I don't like anything that smokes. I'm saving my lungs for dance. And in the barn! Dad smokes cigarettes, but never in the barn. I don't know why I kept it. Basic frugal nature, I guess. *Waste not, want not,* as Grampa would say.

I explain to Mom, but even if she believes me, her freakout already worked its magical damage. Oh, she of little faith!

I retreat to all I've got for a studio, my own private Hide. It's the attic above the milk house. Wood floor, a bunch of junky old pipes and burlap grain sacks. Artifacts from Grampa G.W.'s day. Dusty as hell, but private. It connects to the haymow on its one open side, but even if someone's getting hay they wouldn't notice I'm here, in a corner, writing or stretching. Besides, it's frequently me getting the hay while everyone else is down below doing other chores. I like it up here above it all, warmed enough in winter by ascending cow body heat and cool enough in summer if I open the trapdoor that swings out above the milk-house entrance below. My guess is that's how all these pipes and stuff got in here in the first place, through that trapdoor. If I had the energy, or a friend to help me, I could clean out this place, wall it off from the haymow, set up a barre and a mirror, put a few pillows in the corner for company or audience to sit on, sand and shine the floor, and *voilà*, a real studio. But holy mother of manure, why would I want to ensconce myself here when I'm trying to cut out? I'll deal with the dust only when I need privacy. Safe from the peckings and scratchings of Mrs. Snow.

The point is this: She went through my room. Cleaning, she said, when she knows perfectly well that I, trained by the White Tornado, clean my own room.

So: I go through hers.

Next day, while she is in the barn, I paw through each layer of shabby shirt she owns. Her top drawer of wool socks, her baggy cotton underpants, her one stretched-out, unused sports bra, and an old yellow bra with flaps, for nursing I guess—yech, she kept that thing? I go through polo shirts with *Snow Ridge Farm* embroidered by Grammy and holey T-shirts and a gray hoodie sweater and about a dozen sweatshirts, all with ragged cuffs smelling slightly of iodine. Doesn't she wash her stuff?

And then pants, all the same Levi's jeans, 28-30, all torn in the right knee from repeated kneeling.

I pull the drawer on her nightstand and find a box with a diaphragm, double yech, and a squeezed-out tube of jelly. I close that drawer. I don't touch Dad's nightstand or any of his stuff in their closet.

But I swat her dresses—there are three of them—and a hanging bag with her wedding gown, which I used to play dress-up with. There are shirts and a couple of jackets. And shoes: old sandals she never wears, black heels she wore to Grammy's funeral. I remember the dark holes in the mud at the grave. On the shelf are shoeboxes that I know hold old photos and stuff of our RIP relatives: my half-bro, Timmy; Mom's first hubby, Roland. I vaguely remember Mom showing these boxes to me when I was little, even if she never explained exactly what happened. I have a mental image of Timmy, a curly tousle of dark hair, round face, red cheeks, huge eyes—from these pictures, I guess, because there aren't any others anywhere else in the house. None downstairs on the wall or in the four albums on the bookshelf.

The two shoeboxes on a high shelf are about the most private possessions of hers I can find, not counting the sex stuff, which seems like her outer life, shabby and ugly and totally uninteresting, as ho-hum as the squeeze of a toothpaste tube. But the shoeboxes she tucks away under a little folded blue afghan. I know the boxes are important to her, but even this little shrine seems so dusty and ignored I almost leave it alone. It seems so sad.

Then I think: Mom, you hurt my heart all the time. Nothing you say fits. You don't know me. If you did, you'd know school was fine. You'd know I'm not a pothead.

I take the boxes down and consider. I could light the stove with these. Dust and paper kindle well. I could destroy her old world. I could take her broken heart and turn it to dust. I could give it shock therapy, fire cleansing. I could show her what it feels like to be devalued.

I fling the afghan on top of the black shoes, then think: it's Timmy's blanket, probably, and Timmy's not who I'm mad at. I pick it up, shake off the dust, kiss it, and tuck it onto the high shelf. I carry the boxes to my room because I can't take the air in Mom's stupid, dusty room another minute.

Two cartons: one a Redwing boot box and the other a small Vesey's seed box with a faded label addressed to Roland and Cynthia Wilder, Wild Ridge Farm, Rt. 1, Box 108, E. Greensbrook, Vt. That's not our address anymore. Now, we're Snow Ridge Farm, 108 Jackrabbit Road. Same house but a different street name, handed out when everyone got a 911 address.

Both boxes have the soft, squishy feel of old cardboard, and the tape on the seed box is crackly. I don't think these artifacts get housekeeping attention, not even to shake out their blue crocheted covering. How surprising—not. Cyndy is such a creative homemaker, such a Martha Stewart of Farm America! Pathetic that she only cleans for college kids, for money.

I apologize to Tiny Tim, long-lost little brother. It's not your fault I'm mad at our mother. I don't know how well you knew her, but none of this is your fault, poor boy. Or happy angel, maybe. But nothing about photos cooped up in a dusty case feels free and at ease. We have things in common, kid.

In my room I put the boxes down, close the door, hook the hook, and get comfy *à la seconde* on the floor. Mom's still in the barn. This is schoolwork time and I won't be disturbed unless the phone rings.

I open the shoebox first. Letters and cards wadded together with rubber bands, cracked now and useless as dried-out worms. I pull free a card with a lily and "In Sympathy" on it, and inside a poem and the handwritten words: *Cyndy and Roland, We are so very sorry for your loss. Little Tim wouldn't want you to cry forever though. He was an angel and will be watching over you always. Love, Millie and Fred.*

The Camps. From North Branch. Old as Grampa. I didn't know they knew Timmy. Before I read more I unfold the flaps of the seed box. All photos. Some right side up, some down, all hodge-podge, haphazard, jumbled together as if she just tossed them in without sorting, without a thought. I grab a fistful and see a smiley young woman with long auburn braids holding a baby wrapped in a white blanket up to her face as if she's sniffing a bouquet of flowers. I turn it over. *Timothy George. Sept. 24, 1985.* Same month as me, a Libra, eight years older. He'd be twenty-three. It would be so cool to have an older brother. Not a permanent baby ghost. But these photos hold eternal youth.

There's a photo of Grampa and Grammy sitting on the sofa and, between them, a little boy chewing on the ear of a stuffed cow and looking suspicious.

There's that smiling mother/baby combo again hanging on the arm of a tall, skinny man in a black T-shirt and jeans. He's looking down at her so you can see his long nose but not the expression of his eyes. I'd have to say he fails in the handsome department but passes on the wiry, strong angle. Yup, he looks like a worker.

There's more of those two, even some at their wedding, which appears to be inside St. Jude's. She has on a different dress, prettier and fancier than the one in the closet she let me play with when I was little. Her hair is pulled back and up. Her face is lit with a smile. She looks really young and a little bit chubby. Her face is thinner now.

Most of the other photos are of Baby Timmy. Some have notes on the back: *1 mo., Timmy at 9 mos., T. w/ Santa at fire sta.* The pencil is fading on some of them. *Timmy, 1st steps* is cute: He's outside, naked, fat legs, arms wide, looking very surprised. Baby in the barn sleeping in a basket, Baby in a high chair, Baby in the crook of Roland's arm on a tractor. Yikes, no wonder Mom tucked these away.

Downstairs we have albums with me, Mom and Dad,

Grampa and Grammy, cows, chickens, the Red Sox cats, Whisper, Rat (Walyo's mother), and Walyo, me showing calves at the fair, even Clay and his mom and dad and lots of random kids, school plays, me in the one *Nutcracker* the college did, in *Carmina*, in *Firebird*, in *Giselle*. Mom started over. Maybe she should have thrown these old relics away. They are too sad for words.

Then I wonder, who does she think she is, mooning about, so sad? Isadora Duncan? Does she change Life into Art? Not old Cynny. Unless art is a chore. With Mom, sadness is not art, just a way of looking at the world through dust. Cluck-cluck, skitter away, hide, head under wing.

Well, well, outside my door, here's Walyo, who mostly hangs out like Grampa himself in our house except at night when they go across the driveway to the trailer. Seems old today and waddly, his long toenails clicking across my floor. Hear his wheezy Walyo breath. Emphysema? Farmer's-Dog Lung? Listen, bad-breath bub, I'm going to start calling you Waldo. 'Bout time you got a little respect, seeing as how you'll soon be kicking the bucket with those toenails of yours. I can see it: sleeping on Grampa's floor, one too many rat-chasing dreams, one last leg tremor. Where's Waldo? With Timmy and Roland and Grammy Rose clicking around the Sweet Hereafter, our family farm in the sky.

8

I'VE ALREADY SAID I DON'T REMEMBER BEING BORN EXCEPT
in the metaphorical sense of starting to dance. But I wish I
did. Grammy said everyone was so happy. Dad apparently
danced around the hospital room with me in the crook of his
arm. He wouldn't put me down, and Mom kept murmuring,
"Baby girl, girl, good, mm, good," as if she were drunk with
joy. Grampa announced to the nurses, the midwife, everyone
in sight, "Redheads are beautiful *and* smart."

Grammy, also a redhead, always told that story on my
birthday, up until this September when I turned fifteen. She
should've been here, but she wasn't. I should have been with
her when she died, but I wasn't. Mom sent me away. The
way I see it, Grammy and I are even; Mom and I are not.

While Grammy was sick I hung out with her whenever I could. She liked to hear stories like the ones in *All
Creatures Great and Small*. She had read them all and
nodded and smiled when I read, as if she recognized old
friends on the other side of her closed eyes. She also asked
to hear the Psalms, although I noticed they put her to
sleep. Maybe that was the point. *God is our refuge and our
strength, an ever-present help in trouble. Therefore we will
not fear though the earth give way and the mountains fall
into the sea.* She'd be snoozing peacefully.

I rubbed her feet, always icy cold. They kind of died
before the rest of her and got blue and gnarly when she

stopped walking. But I pretended I was a masseuse for the great Margot Fonteyn and touched each yellow-nailed toe and bone and wormy vein and cracked heel as though it must be softened up and supple enough to slide into satin pointe shoes made by a master cobbler specially for her, in which she would dance to heaven on a shiny floor scented with lavender from her garden. That was a stretch because her feet, objectively speaking, were scarly and lifeless. But she said the Bag Balm I rubbed into them felt good and smelled of happy days.

I didn't mind her smells, not even the diaper smells when it got to that. I clipped roses from her garden; I made teas with her herbs, and a balsam eye pillow so she wouldn't smell death in the room.

I was there with tea before school in the morning; I raced through my chores after so we could read or talk. On the days I danced I got dressed quickly after class and was always ready to go home when Mom arrived to pick me up.

I described my first days at Greensbrook High to Grammy Rose in comic detail because she liked stories. I assured her I was doing well in everything but math, which was true-ish and made her happy, and I told her I was signing up for the Big Brother/Big Sister Program, which also made her happy and would have been true if the meetings weren't after school on Wednesdays, when I had dance. Still, telling her that I was signing up made her smile. "That's my girl," she said. When I looked up from her on the sofa in the stuffy trailer I could see this poem of mine from elementary school that she still had stuck on her fridge.

> *Summer Psalm*
> *Firefly*
> *wandering the*
> *carpet*
> *flashing at*
> *fake flowers of cloth*

She thought every feeble thing I did was *huge*.

Then, stunningly beyond reason, the last weekend Grammy was alive, Mom sent me away. First she called a distant cousin in New Hampshire to ask if I could go there, and she set it up for this almost-stranger to come get me.

"Why?" I asked, totally bewildered.

"No place for you around this sadness," Mom said. Her eyes looked raw from no sleep. The dying was hard on her, I could see that, but she acted as if she owned Grammy, as if Dad and I and even poor Grampa weren't involved.

"You act like you're the only one who cares about her," I said.

It was a discussion she wouldn't have. "I want to stay," I told Dad as clearly as I could. "Why is Mom doing this?"

"She doesn't want you all upset," he said.

"No, no," I said. "That's not it. She wants me out of the way. I have to stay with Grammy."

"Honey, Grammy's not staying long herself."

"That's the point. I need to be here till the end."

"This is hard enough," he said. "Be good now."

They made me go. At the last moment Dad let me call Lacey and he talked to her mother so I could stay there instead of with the cousin. Lacey didn't mind when I cried and cursed all weekend. She even gave me Smirnoff Ice and these little cigars that were gross but distracting.

So Grammy died without me. My mother stole everyone's sadness and wrapped herself in it. Grampa said that was just her way, and he didn't seem to mind. As for being sad himself, he said he and Rosemary had fifty years together and now she'd gone to a better place and wasn't in pain.

That last, I knew, was true, and I guess I was relieved when the trailer smelled like his pipe and Waldo again. But I was left with this: missing Grammy/hating Mom. Here's the problem: if you are cut off from family sadness, are you happy then, or just lonely?

I know what Grampa G.W. said happened. We'd come back from Grammy's funeral Mass, where we'd all blotted our faces with tissues. I needed to talk, so I went out to where Grampa was sitting in Grammy's brown November garden and said, "That was my first funeral."

Grampa laughed, I don't know why, but he didn't say anything, just kept smoking his pipe. I hated that he was sad.

"She had a good life, didn't she?" I said.

He nodded and said, "I enjoyed it," and smiled sweetly. Now he seemed unbearably far away as well as sad, so after ten silent minutes of simmering alone I blurted out, "Did Timmy have a good life?"

"Sure, I guess he did."

"Short, though ..."

"Mm-hmm."

"What happened?"

He finally looked at me. I was praying he wouldn't sigh. He didn't sigh. "You know."

"I know I had a half-brother named Timmy who died, but honestly, no one ever told me what exactly happened. Grampa, you saw how Mom sent me away from Grammy. And how quiet she was today. She won't talk about death."

"No one likes to except maybe a Smith." He laughed. He'd told us how Smith's Funeral Home had tried to interest him in a coffin lined with white cloth fancier than Grammy's wedding dress. But he was saved by the list of instructions she'd written out for him: no coffin, cremation, ashes on her garden.

"Come on, just tell me." I partly figured it might distract him.

And here's his play-by-play.

Well, Timmy was, oh, maybe two, just a little guy, and he was outside the house playing. He had this game where he liked to hide and then jump out at folks saying "Boo!" like he was the scariest devil and you had to act real scared. Well, Roland—you know who he was, don't you?

I nodded. "The first husband," I said.

Yup. Well, he was working on his tractor, an old

Massey Ferguson, just changing the oil and what-not. This was in the spring, late April must have been, getting all set up for spreading manure. I was cleaning out the barn, and Roland—he was going to bring the bucket tractor up soon as he got it fixed and we'd get two spreaders working and really make a dent in the winter pile.

We had a long day ahead, and Donnie, your dad, well, he would come after school like always and help. Rosemary was at her school, and your mother was in the house, doing her house chores after breakfast.

She told Timmy to stay near Daddy, that she'd call him in a few minutes, they'd be going to town for a doctor's appointment. Cyndy had a nasty cold she couldn't shake.

Timmy said at breakfast he'd stay "wif da men," and we all hooted at how that was so cute. But Cyndy said not today, they were too busy, and besides she needed help buying a treat for dinner.

I remember because I almost said, "Let him stay, I'll watch out for him," but I thought again how Cyn was right, the boy was too little for me to keep an eye on all day, and Roland looked kinda peaked already, tired or maybe had some of Cyndy's cold.

I didn't even take li'l Tim to the barn with me like lots of mornings. I just kept my mouth shut and went out. I might have smiled at him, I really don't remember. I partway remember rubbing his head, he had soft dark hair, curly, but maybe I did that another time.

Anyway, I'm working away in the barn, sweeping the

*manger or some such, barn cleaner clanking away, radio on
to whatever the heck Donnie set it on, something loud, and
next thing I know the ambulance is flashing into the driveway
up by the garage. "What the ... ?" I yell to Donnie and we
hightail it down there and my God you don't ever want to see
a thing like that. He must have been playing at hiding from
Roland on the three-point hitch and fell off 'cause Roland was
crying, "I looked behind, I looked behind." But somehow the
baby* was *behind, only hiding must have been, when Roland
started to back up and only stopped when he felt a bump must
have. He never said. Only kept saying, "I looked, I thought
he'd gone in, Cyndy called him, she called him."*

*And she, your mother, was with the tiny boy in the
ambulance by the time I got there. She was holding his little
hand and saying, "Timmy? Timmy?" but I don't think there
was ever hope. Donnie there said it looked to be fast at least.
A quick crush of the chest. Poof, like a candle.*

*And that's just how it felt around here, like dark, fast. I
don't know, Rosemary and me, we felt terrible about Timmy,
he was the sweetest little baby, smart too. But like I said, he
had a good little life, and not much pain, they said.*

*But your mother, that's a different story. It broke our
hearts to see her. She was crushed too and there wasn't a darn
thing anyone could say or do to stop her crying, crying all the
time, for weeks and weeks. I don't suppose anyone will know
what-all they went through. But it was too much for Roland.*

Grampa stopped, shaking his head. I was afraid he
was done.

"What do you mean?" I asked.

You mean your grammy or your dad never told you this?

I shook my head.

Well, a month to the day the boy died, Roland, well, he died too.

"How?" I said, even though I had a rough idea.

You know what I think it was? I think he always loved Cyndy a little too much. He let her rule the roost so to speak, gave her whatever she wanted, gave in easy. She said farm here on her home farm. Okay, he said. Well, he wanted them to go out on their own. But they were hardly done school when they got married. He wanted kids. They didn't have Tim for four, five years! I think to myself that was her doing.

I shouldn't tell you this, but you're a big girl. You know your mother, prickly sometimes. Anyhow, her sun rose and set on that little boy, and I guess Roland knew he couldn't give her what she wanted this time. He felt so guilty, see, and she didn't have time yet to forgive. I'm guessing that's what it was.

He hung hisself. Milked first. Donnie found him hanging from the hay elevator up top when he didn't come down from the mow. He'd thrown down the hay for the night first. I liked Roland. He was a good man.

Donnie, your dad, was just a boy hisself, but he took over. Like God sent him a man's energy. That's about it.

Now in my room I write out Grampa's words as best I can remember them and call it Oral History. I tack it to the wall, my homeschool literary gallery, where Mom will see it if she pokes in here again.

9

TODAY, AFTER MORNING CHORES, AFTER STRETCHING,
I sew a little, read a little, wait for something to happen.

In the afternoon I arrive early at the first "senior" class to be taught by Naheema. I'm early because that's when Mom could take me and because I like to get there before anyone else so I can stretch. In the past it's during times like this when Ursula told me what it takes to be a dancer and when she worked with my problematic, pronating feet. But of course Ursula isn't there today. I'm about to open the studio door when I hear Lacey's voice saying, "Maybe Kit," and Naheema's voice, "Well, I think she wants to be a dancer."

They are talking about me! I pull my hand from the doorknob and lean in to listen.

Lacey: I don't think so. For one thing, there's her boots. You must have noticed the aroma. It's indicative of her family scene. Her parents have cows and no time. Don't you need like a stage mother to help?

Naheema: Maybe. She's a good dancer, a good performer.

Lacey: Mmm … I guess. You should see her show a calf. Great posture, long legs. But I think maybe her feet suck.

Naheema: Hers or the calf's?

They both laugh.

Whoa, what was *that*? I go down the stairs and slump

to the bottom step in shock. How can I enter that room? How could she ruin the day, pollute the studio?

Thaddeus and Joan appear, playing this game the college kids play. "If I were a singer," says Joan, "I'd be Sarah Vaughan."

"Hmm," says Thaddeus, "Nina Simone." He smiles at me and says, "*Vite*, Kit! Up the stairs! If I were an animal, I'd be ... a fox."

"An ox," says big Joan.

A gazelle, I think, although I'm not in the game. A gazelle shot in the back. But I will not let Lacey's stupidity rule. I need to dance. I go up behind Thaddeus and Joan, stamping my boots that are not barn boots and do not smell.

The class itself is very odd. Naheema starts by saying that Ursula's doing okay. She's on some new medicine. She has to give herself shots, apparently, in multiple body parts.

Naheema says that until the new teachers come after winter break, she will be in charge because no one else volunteered. She glares at the other seniors. She says that for the next two weeks we are all both students *and* teachers. Her boyfriend will video the classes—at this point a tall guy with dreads waves from the sidelines—so Ursula can watch and give grades. "We'll do mostly modern since that's what we are doing independent studies on, right? Ursula says carry on with that; do your papers and come to class. The seniors and anyone else who wants to will teach a class in a modern style or your own style and give us a little talk on your dancer. Got it? Any problems?"

She catches my eye. "Kit and Lacey, you girls can do this too or not. Or, if you want to teach a ballet class for us, that's cool too. Or maybe you want to demonstrate for the little kids' class on Saturday—that would be sweet. You let me know. You're not here for credit, so do what you want. But there will be class three times a week. And don't forget the field trip to the dance museum. That's still on."

I'm reminded of grade school when a sub came who didn't know me or what we were doing, so the class just paused for the day. Limbo. I hated that. Lacey is adjusting her hair in the mirror, oblivious of me, of how I hate her. It hurts to look at her.

I try to focus. Any dance class is better than no dance class.

Naheema, dressed all in red, her hair in its million tight braids, tall, long arms and legs relaxed and confident, stands like a healthier, darker, younger version of Ursula, facing us as we scatter along the barre.

The similarity ends.

She says, "Forget the barre. Come to the center, spread out, stand tall, and close your eyes. Breathe deep. Say what I say, call and response." Then she chants something like this:

We ask ... (We sing back, "We ask")

Humbly ... ("Humbly")

Isadora ... ("Isadora")

Ruth Martha Mary Hanya Doris ... ("RuthMartha MaryHanyaDoris")

Helen Katherine Pearl Anna ... ("HelenKatherine PearlAnna")

Your blessings on our dance.

She says we are thanking the ancestors. "Female ones," Thaddeus murmurs. Someone laughs.

Lacey rolls her eyes at me. She's never been a Naheema fan. Says she's *too confident.* I pretend I don't notice. She doesn't know I heard her disparage me. I think Naheema is majestic.

She calls it a modern class based on Graham. Bare feet, which I like; her friend films the class, another guy drums. I like using my back. We start seated on the floor doing bounces, stretches, spirals, using contraction and release, which N. demonstrates vividly with her long and limber torso. Who knew she could dance like this? Or does whoever teaches always look good because they have to?

We never touch the barre. Everything in the center and simple, *pliés, tendus,* but with a twist, this spiral thing going on in the back that makes me feel Whisper-esque. We end with simple prances, triplets, then skips and leaps on three. Very clean and lifted and crisp.

I leave feeling my hips as high as my waist and my legs long, long, stretching down from there, coltish and loose. Who knew she knew this? Ballet is like a uniform we all wear, and underneath N.'s, *voilà!* I wonder what is under my uniform. Probably more ballet.

10

ADD THEM UP: (1) NO SCHOOL, (2) NO URSULA, (3) DEAD
half-brother, (4) dead Grammy, (5) dead friendship. I could
be comatose with misery.

The days are short, cold, dark, and dreary. I begin to
hallucinate while I'm standing at the Harvestore unloader
with my thumb pressing the On button. This day, because
it's colder than hell (meaning way cold rather than a
pleasant relief from fire and brimstone), my feet and hands
are icy and I can't feel my face. Weather reports keep prom-
ising more snow, but all we get today is deep freeze. The silo
unloader is groaningly slow as it chips off shards of frozen
haylage. Supposed to be a ten-minute job. Today it takes ten
times longer.

I'm using my thumb so my other fingers can curl
together for warmth in the palm of my work glove. Why
can't this button just stay on without being held down? Dad
told me why: so you watch this machine every minute and
so it turns off immediately if you or anyone gets caught in
the chain, which, apparently, could make quite a mess.

Actually, in spite of the child-endangerment aspect, I
love this setup: unloading haylage from silo, unloader into
conveyor, conveyor carrying chop to feed cart, feed cart
spewing feed down the aisle of cow heads, heads eating,
feed ruminating, milk made in mammary glands, teats
squirting milk into claws, hoses leading to pipeline, pipe-

line carrying warm milk to bulk tank, bulk tank cooling, truck pumping milk from tank and hauling it away to feed a hundred people. Not to mention bovine butts squirting manure into gutters, gutter cleaner moving the gunk from barn to spreader, spreader flinging fertilizer onto fields, fields making more haylage, which goes into the silo, which I unload.

I love the flow, the cycles, the simplicity of the machines. When they work. I love being a piece of the process, a catalyst, a cog. When it works.

It's like a dance class. Barre before center; *pliés* before *tendus* before *dégagés*. As Grampa says, *First things first, next is next.* Peaceful and purposeful work. If only it weren't so freakin' cold.

So I'm standing there, thinking all this, and to keep from solidifying into ice sculpture I'm doing *pliés* and *tendus*, slowly and as fully as I can with my thumb pushing the On button.

Clay appears at the stable door by the feed cart. There's steam around him where the cold is hitting the warmer barn air. He's grinning at me and holding his pinkie delicately upraised and his face in actually elegant *épaulement*. He squats his version of a *plié*.

I don't take it personally. I figure he just can't think what else to say. "Gotta move or I'll freeze," I say through shivery lips.

He comes down into the shed. Behind me. Reaches over my shoulder, replaces my thumb with his red chapped naked finger, wraps his other arm around me, and pulls me close. "I'll warm you," he says.

Not! That didn't happen.

This happened: I blushed when I saw his ballet imitation. Then I said, "Gotta move or I'll freeze," and he said, "Guess so" and "Want me to finish that? It's slow," and I said, "Sure, I'll start milking," and he said, "Okay," and we switched places. Okey-dokey. So. I was warm going in and out between the cows and bending my knees to milk, but not so warm as I might have been ...

Yikes, what am I, a romance writer? Am I going crazy from confinement?

I don't even really know Clay, much less like him. He has stupid friends like Mike, whose smoking in the barn led to the room searches by Mom and by me. I wonder what Clay sees in the idiot. He rides over with Clay on snow machines sometimes. Clay stays to work; I don't know where Mike goes from here, but he goes there fast. I can hear him roaring away from inside the barn over the sound of the gutter cleaner, radio, and silo unloader. And I can smell the gaggy gas fumes, worse than silage or manure.

Then last week I'm skiing, first time this year, on the trail between our farm and Clay's Hide. By the side of the cabin, in new snow, in big, frozen, yellowish letters, is M I K E —a dopey dog marking his spot. God!

"Clay," I said the next day, "did you see that Mike pissed his name in the snow by your camp?"

"No," he said.

"Why would he do a dumb thing like that?" I said.

Clay shrugged. "Gotta go, you gotta go."

"Don't you think it's gross? He couldn't wait till he got to your house, or at least go in the bushes?"

Loyal as oil, he wouldn't disown that idiot. He just smiled. "It's supposed to snow later. It'll cover over."

So I can't really like Clay. I can see it now: Me and Clay are curled together on a braided rug by a fire of our own, playing Scrabble, no, reading poetry, okay, watching *Life of Brian*. Mike's face appears, lips pushed against the window, eyes crossed crazily.

"Eh, Clay," he calls through the window over our music and the crunch of the fire, "got a beer?"

If that's where I'm headed, I'm doomed.

11

DAD INTERRUPTS MY DESCENT INTO MADNESS BY TAKING
me on a field trip to check out a robotic milking machine
on a farm east of Montreal. He's always trying to prevent
the demise of our family farm—against the odds, I might
add. Why not go, I figure. Not a dance day, and besides,
Lacey has violated the studio as a peaceful place for me. My
plan is to retaliate with icy silence.

The silence between Dad and me, on the other hand,
is companionable. After driving for a while we arrive at an
"open house" run by the manufacturer Lely. Us and lots of
other farmers, some French, some American. I can hardly
understand the extension guy who is doing most of the
talking. But the technicians are younger, Dutch, and they
speak English to me while smiling and offering doughnuts.
Dad keeps nodding and running his hand over his chin.
Every now and then he'll wink and smile at me too, to keep
me included, I guess.

But I don't see how the whole high-tech jibber-jabber
includes us anyway. These robots "work" in a free-stall barn
doing sixty-five cows per hour. We don't even have a free-
stall. We milk in a tie-stall barn doing thirty to forty cows
per hour. That's just the point, Dad says on the way home.
We'll build a new barn, get off our knees.

The robot is like a stainless-steel box that does all these
things: figures feed, dips teats, puts the unit on, takes it off,

dips again, totally auto. The cows go to it on their own, whenever they want, getting grain at the same time to their computer-determined personal limit.

Granted, it seems to work; the cows we saw were calm and content. But I wouldn't want it. I like being side by side with the cows even if I'm squeezed hip to hip, cheek to cheek. It's a dance.

"Don't you want to be a partner with the cows?" I ask Dad. "Not a machine."

"Exactly," he says. "Let the robot be the machine! We'll have time for other things. I can manage, hunt, take a breath; your mother can save her back; you can dance, be a kid."

Out of the blue I think of Timmy. He'd have the time of his life. Boys love machines.

"Dad, do you wish you had a son?" I say. "One that wants to farm?"

"What are you talking about? I like girls." He winks at me. I know he means the cows, his "girls."

"Dad, are you disappointed I don't want to farm?"

"You don't?"

"Come on." I punch his arm. "Don't joke."

"No, really, does anyone at age fourteen know what they want?"

"Fifteen. And yes. Probably dance. I mean, I'm not sure."

"Kitty, let's just put one foot in front of the other and not worry about later too much. You can do what you want. Pretty much."

"Within reason."

"Dead right," Dad says.

As French signs and flat fields rush by, I suddenly feel scattered. If I really wanted to dance I'd run away and do it, not fritter away my youth going to farm-robot meetings with my dad. Maybe I'm not single-minded enough. Maybe I'm ADHD, although in that department I was always outshone by standouts like Ryan Weston, so I've never been diagnosed. Besides, my grades were fine and I never knifed anyone, so, hey, no problem. I never, to the best of my memory, even knifed anyone figuratively, like a certain former friend.

But maybe the dance studio is the only place I can really focus. The barn is clearly the only place where Dad focuses. He's fiddling with the radio to find a hockey game, one staticky station after the next. He pauses, thank God, to use both hands going around a curve. A guy on the radio is talking about when something good becomes bad. He calls it "jumping the shark" when you take a foolish risk and your luck changes.

"Ouch," Dad says.

"Did you jump the shark when you married Mom and had me?" The question pops out of me.

"Why would you think a thing like that?" he says, sounding genuinely puzzled.

Conversation dangles and Dad changes the station again. A weather report warns of snow coming, the wheel turns, life goes on. I don't really want to ruin things for Dad if he likes his life. I just wonder.

Later that night, after dinner—during which he jabbered about robots and Mom harped on the ridiculous cost—Dad does dishes. I'm reading in the newspaper about another National Guard unit going to Iraq. Dad goes, "The suds held for the whole time!" He sounds delighted. The suds held! Small stuff makes him happy. You gotta admire that.

Then he keeps changing dusty tapes in our boomless box: *West Side Story*? Reject. Willie Nelson? No. Fred Eaglesmith? Ah! Mom's drying pots and wiping the counter, but he grabs her and galumphs around the floor with her while she's whining, "Don, I need to finish!" Party pooper. Progress preventer. Sweet simpleton, he doesn't care.

I retreat to my room with the phone, then remember I'm not talking to Lacey. You do not suck, I tell my feet. Whisper curls on my bed, napping. I switch on my radio and lie down with my face in Whisper's fur. I can just hear Lacey: *Radio, Kit? God, you need an iPod like normal people.* What's playing is *Appalachian Spring*, even though it's the tail end of fall, because today is December 2, Aaron Copland's birth or death day, I didn't hear which. Ursula adores this music, has played parts of it in class. She once showed us an old film of the Martha Graham dance he wrote it for. She sang scattered words to one section: *'Tis a gift to be simple, 'tis a gift to be free … Dance, dance wherever you may be.* A gift that is eluding me …

Whisper is licking my hair, tending the fire in my head. To be simple or to be free, simple or free, that is the question.

12

FIRST SUNDAY OF ADVENT WE TREK TO GOD'S HOUSE, JUST
Mom and me. I don't really know why I go when Mom asks
me. Maybe to pray for deliverance. Dad does chores, *bien
sûr*. Grampa reads the Bible and talks about going with
Roberta to a Kingdom Hall. He reads this from Psalms at
breakfast before we go: "Here is my description of a truly
happy land where Jehovah is God: Sons vigorous and tall as
growing plants. Daughters of graceful beauty like the pillars
of a palace wall." He smiles at Mom. "Barns full to the brim
with crops of every kind. Sheep by the thousands out in
our fields—well, never mind that. Oxen loaded down with
produce. No enemy attacking the walls, but peace everywhere. No crime in our streets. Happy are those whose God
is Jehovah."

"Sounds great, Grampa," I say. I see the appeal to a guy
like him, but I notice he's reading from my Children's Bible,
not the one Roberta brought over. Could it matter?

I guess I go to St. Jude's with Mom because I'm up
anyway and I always went with Grammy. Saint Jude, the
patron of hopeless cases, seems an excellent choice to inter-
cede with God on my behalf. Besides, I like the ritual of
stand/sit/kneel. Madeline Gomez, who plays the organ and
leads the singing, has an incredible voice. She could be a
pro but she sings at rinky-dink St. Jude's instead and works
at the Mobil.

We have come to tell our story, we have come to break bread.

There are lovely roses on the altar. With thorns, I imagine. Imagination can be a thorn in my side. Sometimes like now during the boring sermon I start to imagine Timmy's voice. I imagine what he would write about my performance last year. I jot it on the missalette. *Me and Mom and Dad went to a balay. It was called Gizelle. My sister was in it. She is a balarina. She had pointy shoes and her dress was pooffy and a white thing was on her head. It was okay. Kitty was pretty. I gave her flowers Mom said to.*

Did anyone give me flowers for real at the performance last spring? Negative. Mom, Dad, and Grampa got there late because the milk tester came and chores take longer on test night. Besides, it was not long after Grammy's funeral. Maybe giving me flowers would have reminded Mom of that.

Mom nudges me with her elbow, presumably for not listening to the sermon.

I receive Communion feeling blameless, in spite of my tendency to embellish the truth and harbor grudges. Imagination is no lie, no sin, and neither is standing up for yourself. I'm sure of it. Bread = Jesus' body, Jesus = God, anybody = what they eat, my body = bread at the moment, my body = Jesus' body. I go no further. Not blasphemy, just thinking. Church is a good place for thinking new thoughts. Like how Mom in spite of her faults is a very good kneeler. Other people her age sag their butts. But she's upright with great posture in this context. Course I guess she practices while she's milking or when she's weeding in the garden. She's all about kneeling. That Martha Graham dance also featured some awesome kneeling. For the half hour Mass takes, Mom doesn't sag. Or nag, except without words.

13

THE TEACH-YOURSELF PLAN IS INCREDIBLY BORING. IT'D be easier online, but Mama Snow's Homeschool lacks all but an ancient computer Grammy got at a yard sale, thinking it would be good for farm records and for me to type papers. I don't love blinking screens or long to IM, but the Internet would make those workbooks quicker and more fun. Mom says computers are "one window to greediness." What?! Dad and I are together on this. His robots will need to run by computer. I ask if she knows she's a Luddite. She says, "Oh, Kit," and doesn't answer the question.

One of the homeschooling books Mom got says, "Fill in the blank: I want to learn _____."

Weeell, I want to learn to surf, to do triple pirouettes, to grow avocados and apricots, which I love. I want to learn to dance like Martha Graham and Margot Fonteyn and Judith Jamison, all three of whose tapes I saw recently. No, I don't want to look like any of them. I want to be completely original, the greatest *something* ever. I don't know what yet. But I can't just hang around wasting time, giving Mom and Dad these years. They are addicted to sadness and love, she and Dad. Husband number one, he blows things big-time. What does she do? Goes gaga for the first guy's hired man. A kid. A boy. Still gaga, in that she works with him all day, every day. Except for her brief independent stints as bathroom washer for rich kids. Manure scraper, toilet scrubber—God, Mom, what you must think of yourself! Get a life. No, just let *me* have a life!

Christmas is coming and I'm not excited, because that's all I want, a life. Hmm, I also want laser surgery so I don't have to wear glasses like a geezer or contacts like little fake patch-ups for my eyes.

This is what I got for Christmas last year: From Dad, a framed poster of a dancer. From the knees down, two feet in fifth position, a crisscross, space like diamonds between the ankles and the knees, torn leg warmers with holes like Dad's ripped sweaters, duct tape wrapped around the toes of the slippers. Surely Dad felt we shared a bond. From Mom I got a flannel nightgown and socks. Oh, and a leather show halter she said I wanted, which was formerly true, I guess. On Christmas morning, however, it seemed like a thinly disguised leash for me.

That was it last Christmas. The first Christmas without Grammy. We prayed a lot.

Suddenly it's serious winter. Flash freeze and snow. My favorite part of today was skiing to and from the barn in the butt-freezing cold. I mean *cold*. Ten below zero tonight, Dad says. But at choretime it wasn't that bad. Sunny. Windy, though. Anyway, I skied all the way through the sugarbush—that's about a half-mile detour to go the hundred yards from the house to the barn. Clay made a trail with his Arctic Cat when he went to clear a few trees from the logging road for Dad. It worked slick for me. Climbing all the way up was a workout, and gliding down was bliss.

I met Dad by the milk-house steps and kicked off my skis. We went in together, and together we stopped to wipe off our fogged-up glasses. "What a pair we are," he said. "Two blind bats."

Tonight it felt weird doing chores like I'm Dad's crony. Him humming country, thinking I'm his little pumpkin or some figment of his nostalgic parent brain, me just wishing I'd put in my contacts, even if the chaff and grain dust makes that a grim plan. I don't mind chores. I like the cows and the ritual dances of levering bales to feed and scooping grain, of bending and rising, of squeezing between warm bodies. But today it feels so middle-aged. Clay left early, there are no new calves, and Mom's not there to partner with Dad and let me be free. Because the roads were so bad she left late to clean and I sure as hell didn't want to go with her. To be at the college now and not be at the studio is torture! Sometimes I see Naheema or Henry or Sarah from class, and there I am mopping or dusting. *Très* weird.

It is dark of course when we get done. I say I'm gonna ski the loop home. Dad says go on, he has a few things to finish up, Moonshine to treat. The whole time that I'm skiing through the quiet still cold, no wind in the woods, the barn lights are showing through the trees. I'd have to ski all the way to The Hide to escape the lights from the barn. When I get to our porch, the barn lights flick off, and here comes Dad trudging down the hill waving the beacon of a cigarette. He just happens to be done when I am. Blatant or what. Is he my lighthouse? My hero? My guardian? My jailer? I love him, but sometimes it's so annoying how he's always around.

As the days slide closer to the solstice it's hard for me to get out of bed. The morning is dark and cold. There's a sameness to the days. I wonder what matters. I mean, if I get up now at five-thirty or in half an hour at six, it matters. In that time I could eat breakfast, take a shower, feed Waldo and Whisper. Or I could stretch. Or do a mini-barre. Or I could sleep those thirty minutes and be better psyched for the rest of the day. If I do one thing or the other it changes the world. Atoms move in different ways.

Say I get up now. I'll be cold, so I'll run to the bathroom and turn on hot water in the shower. The furnace will need to heat more water. The furnace will run, using oil. We'll need to buy more oil sooner. Evarts Energy will send a bill, which Mom will pay, furrowing her brow as she does, which will age Mom. Evarts Energy will join the chorus pushing to stay in Iraq to help us get oil. The bathroom steam will increase the mildew on the ceiling, which I will be asked to clean with stinky spray chemicals, which will send me to an early grave.

If I stay in bed longer, I'll stay warm from simple pure body heat. When I do get up I'll have to hurry to feed the chickens and get my other stuff done, and that also will warm me up. Better I stay in bed, save oil, save Mom's stress level, prevent war, prolong my life.

I turn over and snuggle into my warm nest. I sigh deeply. The door creaks gently. I hear firm footfalls. *Thum thum thum thum.* A rush of cool air, scent of balsam/ wood smoke. Strong hands on my neck, shoulders, under the covers. Cool, but as they work gently, firmly down my back, heat begins to course through my body, my belly, my thighs, the secret recesses in between. I feel his breath on my neck. I smile. Sensuously luxuriating in his touch I turn toward him.

There is no one there, *bien sûr*. Now I really am running late with nothing to show for my time but an empty, impossible fantasy. Does it matter? It must. How?

When I get to the barn Mom starts right in. "You know, Kitty, homeschooling does not mean sleeping in every day. You can learn what you want, but you have to get on a routine." She wants to fight, I know she does, so I don't even begin to say for the hundredth time that I know she wants me to go to St. Rose.

Grampa chimes in as he stands leaning on the hoe he's using to scrape manure. "Dilly-dally brings night as fast as hurry-scurry."

"Oh, Dad," Mom says, putting her shoulder to Sweetpea and attaching a milker, "you're not helping."

I smile at him; I wonder where he gets his material. "Is that in the Bible?" I say.

"Should be," he says.

"You going to Bible study with Roberta tonight?" I ask him.

"Might," he says.

"You like her, don't you?" I say. I know this train of thought bugs Mom, who pretends she's not listening and tinkers with cows that don't need it.

"Well, she's an interesting lady."

"Like how interesting?"

"Oh, you know, she plays clarinet in the Hope Springs Band."

"As interesting as Grammy Rose?" I ask, feeling mean.

"No." He shakes his head. "No. Rosemary was not interesting; she was my better half. Loving is different. Interesting is curious-like."

"Doesn't interest turn into love?" I can't resist.

"Not so much, I don't think, but I don't really know a thing about it." Grampa smiles and heads down the walkway, sweeping.

I wonder. One thing I hated about school was Bruce Hutchins, who would be seen only with built blond girls with perfect skin, of whom there are about ten in the whole school of eight hundred. And he dated them all in a row as though they were a show string he was acquiring for the fair. Only he would bomb at showmanship because he's clearly more interested in showing himself than his "animals." *What a great bod I've got. Don't I have a great bod? Aren't I hot?* The word *swagger* was invented for him. For him and for roosters. Everything outward, feathers and spurs, nothing inside. Handsome and who cares. I'm reading this book we have about chickens, and it calls roosters "ambient genitals." *Ambient* is such a great word. I want to tell Lacey. I'm thinking of taking the high road and forgiving her so we can talk.

So Grampa is right. More fun to be interested than to be in love. Well, he didn't say that, I'm extrapolating. But he seems happy about Roberta and he's always cheery with Mom.

"Grampa," I ask when we're alone in the milk house finishing up chores, "is Mom interesting?"

"Well ..." He pauses at the sink. "She's a tough bird. You seen her doctor the cows, giving shots and such. Ever seen a cow kick her? You won't. And keeping the books and her business. It's beyond me. She figures out a lot and she ain't had things easy. You got to remember that."

He flicks off the lights and we head down to the house for supper. *Remember that. Remember that.* What if I'm not interested in remembering?

At supper I slide beef chunks to one side, away from the stewed veggies I'll eat. Mom says, "When I was little, Grammy said I had to eat every bite on my plate because there were children starving in China. Right, G.W.?"

This is the sort of clichéd thing she calls conversation.

"Am I little?" I ask.

"You need to eat for the strength to work, to put milk in other people's glasses. So we get money to buy stuff we want, like pointe shoes."

Ouch!

Grampa goes, "I'll say this: no food, no life."

"Besides," she says to me, ignoring him, "you don't want to get anorexic."

That's it. I stand up and pinch an inch of my muscled arm. "Do I look anorexic?"

She shakes her head, squinches her eyes closed, and rubs them. I sit down, thinking about when Grammy stopped eating toward the end, and then Grampa winks at me and says, "So, thank God and Cyndy for this fine meal."

Dad clears his throat and says, "Good food is second only to love as a reason to live. Eat, drink, and be merry—right, G.W.?—for tomorrow you die. *Carpe diem.* Isn't that in the Bible?"

Grampa chortles along, so cooperative. You can't say they don't try.

Mom scowls at my rejected beef.

14

Big day. Today marked one year of periods. At first I was glad because I'd waited so long for it. Late bloomer, Mom told me. She made me the same raspberry-leaf tea Grammy had made her.

Jubilation passed. I hadn't factored in the mess, how heavy I would feel. Once in a while would be okay, but every month! I once heard Ursula shout out, "Dancers don't have periods!"—by which she meant that some of the kids should stop complaining about cramps, headaches, being tired, etc. She meant: *Shut up and dance.* I would never whine out loud about it. You always feel better anyway if you keep moving and don't brood. Only today, while Naheema talked, I was leaking even with a Super that I just put in before class. After, the string was a red wick and my leotard crotch was damp with a warm, earthy smell. Not a bad smell; it's barnlike. But private. I'm glad I was wearing black, and I'm glad we didn't do many big jumps. I had to keep thinking about pulling up through my center to contract.

But now I'm home, and even though I'm all showered and everything, drugged with a pain pill because my gut feels like an achy lagoon, even so, I'm glad to put on overalls and boots and slog through the barn. Here I can bleed, here I can smell, here I can ache. I sit on a bale and rub my belly. Peppermint nudges my waist. Her cow breath is my breath. No holding anything in. Here we snort. They pee, they poop, they push out calves, they bleed off after heat. My blood relatives. Here I can rest, I can flow. I almost fall asleep. Mom jars me awake—"Hey, Kitty"—and helps feed out the bale.

I'm not my usual peppy self. That's what periods do. Or maybe it was the class today or the time I spent alone in the studio before anyone else arrived.

I've always loved the studio. Worn but smooth dark floorboards creak and seem as old as my house. The mirrors reflecting light from high windows above the barre make their dullness shine. I see the sky when I arch back, stretching. I hear students laughing as they change classes, I hear the cedars outside blowing against the windows. Dancers are a minority at Hope Springs; ballet is not exactly the hottest class on campus. Ursula says no one realizes how beautiful we are. We judge ourselves by the mirror and by how we feel. We look at ourselves and at an image somewhere beyond the room, beyond the sky, close to the music, to heaven. Something on somebody always hurts, maybe me least of all, but I'm the youngest, stronger because I work a lot—not work out, just work. Ursula says we're marginal because there's no major in dance. We're under Phys Ed, replaceable by pilates or yoga in the administrative mind. We are forgotten, we are in church, we are elite, focused, quiet, sweating.

Ursula was exquisite when she was here. She sang to us, she whispered, she shouted, she pleaded with us and despaired. She cajoled. Her hair was pulled to a bun, not tight like some of ours but wispy, breathy, lyrical, as if always in a land of breeze. She got hot. She brushed the air often with a hand fan. Her neck was a flower stem, her white face a tired peony. When she tired, when we tired her, she sat in a folding chair.

At one end of the studio is a tiny office where Argus, her collie, slept during class. I miss him too. It's my dream of a room with pictures of famous dancers on the walls, of Ursula in a group of Egyptian-looking dancers, in a white dress, or looking like an Amazon in a black unitard in some old dance with an intense guy in tights, no shirt, reaching for her. In another photo she's a childlike sylph in pointe shoes. She says she was never a star, but I can't believe that. There's enough in the pictures alone to take my breath away, fill me with the lighter air of inspiration.

Lacey thinks she should hang up pictures of her students, us and the college kids, in our performances. Why should she? She's not our mother. We might have looked pretty good in our mini-versions of *Giselle* or *Firebird*, but not so good as Martha Graham, Mary Wigman, Maria Tallchief, Merce Cunningham, Margot Fonteyn, and Mikhail Baryshnikov. Anyway, our names don't start with M.

On Ursula's desk above paper-stuffed pigeonholes are photos of her children, Helga and Christian, when they were little. I used to see them around; they're older than me, but now I think they mostly live with their father in Boston. Or maybe they're on their own. I don't really know. I wonder if they visit, now that she's sick.

Naheema's class today was more or less the same, Graham-ish. Only first Thaddeus said he wanted to lead the thanksgiving chant to the ancestors. Naheema narrowed her eyes to a slit and gave a thin, one-sided smile, took a breath, and closed her eyes. I closed mine. He recited many men's names. I know Balanchine. And Stravinsky. Who is Mark Morris? He ended with *"Merci."*

When I opened my eyes Naheema was smiling. "Hmm, that's some soup you made of them boys, and some of them still among the living. But thank you, Thad."

I don't know half of them or N.'s "mothers" either. But learning about them becomes my mission. I borrow some of Ursula's books and stay up till two a.m. reading.

During the next two weeks all the seniors teach classes, some better than others. Improvisation with Thaddeus is weird but fun. He gives us problems to solve: *Use the floor as a focal point and tool. Hold it, sink into it, push it away, stick to it, trip on it, take off from it but be aware of returning to it. Never ignore the floor; be conscious of body movement and others only in relation to the floor. Use your whole body, not just feet and legs.* We use no music but our breath and floor sounds: creaks, groans, thuds, footsteps. We end class with cartwheels, handstands, and walk-overs, which Thaddeus is very good at. He says he's a Taurus, very centered and grounded. I come out of his class laughing.

Joan teaches tap, which is hysterical since only two people have tap shoes. A few kids get pairs she borrowed from the theater department, but not me. Joan herself is brilliant. Again, you'd never have guessed. She's large, lumpy, I guess you could say, and I never really looked at her in ballet. But she can move her feet to rhythms almost before I hear them. Exciting. I just wish I'd had the right shoes. Even my Chippewas would be better than running shoes, way too sticky.

Eveline brings back the drummer and distributes an armload of borrowed sarongs for us to dress up in. She's brought along some of her friends from the African Dance Group. The energy is crazy and the room gets steamy enough to fog the windows, but I never know exactly what step we are doing. She tells me at one point not to think so much, which makes me want to leave. But I have never, ever left a dance class before the bitter end, never even considered it before, so I don't and things get marginally better. Lacey, however, keeps coming over to me and saying, *Isn't this awesome?* That annoys me and makes me super self-conscious until the very end, when we are supposed to dance alone one by one to thank the drummer. I don't know what to do except listen to the drum and move with the sound. I guess I do okay because Eveline whoops and claps, although she does for everyone, I think.

Tall, gawky Michelle, with black-rimmed glasses, says she wants her band, Cabin Fever, to come and do a contradance. She'll teach the dances; we can invite lots of people, charge admission, and give the money to Ursula.

There is eye rolling at that, and at first Naheema tells

Michelle that if she wants credit she'll have to teach a normal class they can tape for Ursula to see. Lacey mutters to me under her breath, "Who died and made her God?" which makes no sense at all. I pretend I don't hear.

But they finally decide why *not* do a contradance benefit for Ursula. Michelle says she guarantees it will attract more people than an evening of improvising with the floor. Everyone laughs at Thaddeus, even Thaddeus. The benefit is set for January, the first weekend after winter break.

15

LAST CLASS BEFORE CHRISTMAS IS THE FIELD TRIP, A three-hour drive to the National Dance Museum in Saratoga Springs. Lacey couldn't come because of exams, so it is just little old me and eight college kids in a Hope Springs van.

Mom, of course, was reluctant to let me go. "Crazy to go so far in a day" is how she beat around the bush hiding her true feelings. Fortunately, she happened to run into Ursula and Naheema outside the building she was cleaning, and they convinced her.

Mom said Ursula looked pale and tired. "Grammy would recommend dandelion and dock for strength. I'll bring her some. But that Nay-he-ma seems like a very polite and responsible girl, with a very unusual name, don't you think?"

The actual selling point, I suspect, was Ursula's assurance that N. would share the driving with Henry Rouleau, who also drives the ambulance for the Hope Springs Rescue Squad. That kind of credential impresses Mom.

She gets me there early. I snag the window seat right behind N., who starts off at the wheel with Henry beside her shuffling CDs.

Thaddeus arrives just as we are pulling out and slides into the empty seat next to me. He taps my leg and says, "Good work." He waves toward Naheema. "Sally forth," he says. Half the time I don't understand what he's talking about, like now, so I giggle like a little kid. He offers me a white tablet of gum.

I'd been nervous about the trip, since I don't do anything with them but dance, and I'm so much younger, not to mention *sheltered* by Madame Kid-Curator. I shouldn't have worried. For three hours T. has me laughing, answering his questions, and listening to him argue, sing, swat Henry on the head. Joan and Eveline, ears plugged to iPods, eyes closed, seem to snooze in the seats behind me. Michelle, next to them, reads and takes notes. Others way in the back talk or listen to music or eat stuff.

Up front it's showtime. T. sings along with the tune:

I wish I knew how it would feel to be free
I wish I could break all the chains holding me

"That's beautiful," I say, and T. suddenly grabs both my arms, pulls me to face him, and breathes, "I love Nina Simone." I see my surprised face in his huge brown eyes. He releases me and sits back smiling; he mimes holding a microphone and says in a deep voice, "Tell me, Kit, who the hell are you? Why isn't a nice girl like you in high school?"

I tell him my saga, more or less. "High school sucks anyway, unless you're into balls," he says. "Sports, you know." He gets me talking about the farm. Do we milk by hand (no), could he get raw milk (in our kitchen only, we ship the rest to get pasteurized), do we use BST or GMOs (no), can I drive a tractor (yes, duh), do we ever have to go to a grocery store (omigod yes), and so forth. I feel like some rare exotic animal, more the center of attention than when I was Clara for two performances of an abbreviated *Nutcracker* three years ago.

Thaddeus and Henry and Naheema want to hear things I never talk about. Like how long my family has owned the land. They ask about Grampa and think it's really funny his name is George Washington. T. asks, do I know the famous George Washington was homeschooled? Henry says *he* was homeschooled for two years after he got hassled at Greensbrook High. He doesn't say why he got hassled. Henry does say he's really sorry about my grandmother and that she was the best cook at school; his mother sometimes got herbs from her and said she was a great healer. My eyes fill; I say, "Yeah." I begin to feel the most normal I have in ages. Maybe my life isn't completely bizarre.

I only vaguely notice that we've crossed the lake border into New York State when N. stops to switch drivers at the Fort Ann Quik Stop. There's no fort in sight, just gas stations and "collectible" junk shops, lots of billboards advertising stuff, including one with just a huge phone number. I laugh and say, "Whose phone number?"

"The guy who wants to rent out the billboard," T. says. Now I feel dumb.

Henry drives us on a bigger highway now, past an amusement park, The Great Escape, closed for the season. I've heard of it, never been there. Enormous roller-coaster tracks look like dormant steel dragons, lots more thrilling than the puny rides we get at Field Days. I'd say so but I feel we've had enough of my quaint background. And the guys are on to other topics: a party at Ryder House, a Godhead song about forever locked something, and T. saying he heard two bull moose were found in New Hampshire recently, dead because they locked antlers fighting and couldn't separate. An exhibit of them, called "Forever Locked," is traveling around New England. Naheema winces, says, "Males!" She starts reading from MapQuest to Henry. He zooms along the highway, faster now, and finally cruises past the Saratoga racetrack T. points out to me and through a town four times the size of Greensbrook, five times the size of Hope Springs, lined with coffee and clothing shops. We arrive with a lurch at the museum, "a former bathhouse on the edge of Saratoga Spa State Park," Naheema reads from a flyer. Like I know what a bathhouse is.

Inside, we have the echoing hallways almost to ourselves. Naheema speaks in a dignified way to the gray-haired woman at the reception window, awing her, I imagine. Elegant in her patchwork silk jacket and tight black pants, Naheema looks enough like a dancer to make up for the sloppier members of our group. I try to stand tall. I breathe something sacred in the space, whether from bathers or dancers I don't know. Goose bumps prickle my arms.

I lose my companions T. and Henry at the Paul Taylor exhibit in honor of his fifty years in dance. I follow most of the others to an exhibit called "Dancing Rebels: The New Dance Group," about modern dancers and choreographers in the 1930s and 40s. *Dance Is a Weapon in the Class Struggle*, a big poster proclaims. If this were a high school trip, the teacher would be reading to us and most kids would be checking out the bathrooms or sneaking a smoke outside. Naheema seems mesmerized by a video of a Donald McKayle dance where a gorgeous black woman carves air to the spoken words, *Though the Virgin be white / Paint little black angels for me / For they too go to heaven.* Eveline and Joan are looking at pictures of the Katherine Dunham we chanted about. Nearby I watch an old film called *Strange Hero*—Daniel Nagrin dancing with a cigarette and reminding me of Dad. Goose bumps again.

Ursula had described the exhibit as "political," but it seems to me more about everyday dance. Familiar somehow. But not ballet.

I drift eventually to a section about Martha Graham, where black-and-white photos are matched with quotes of hers that seem also deeply familiar.

We learn by practice ...

Movement never lies. It is a barometer telling the state of the soul's weather to all who can read it.

I'd like to be known as a storyteller. I have a holy attitude toward books. If I was stranded on a desert island I'd only need two, the dictionary and the Bible. Words are magical and beautiful.

In the photos of her and her dancers, the bodies, especially the men's, look like sculpture, almost naked. The women are draped and powerful-looking, like goddesses or saints. I shiver, overwhelmed by beauty and gospel messages targeted at me.

I find a resting place: a bench by a screen where you can push a button to see old clips of famous dancers. I push the top one: Doris Humphrey, "Air for the G String." Five women gliding and swooping in patterns to music sounding like my heartbeat. I push the button over and over, feeling like I'm in church. "Bach," T. whispers in my ear as he pauses behind me. This is heaven.

There is some ballet stuff, a few costumes, Balanchine quotes and photos in another room like a distant relative. Clearly not the focus of the featured exhibit. The others barely glance in. And I too keep gravitating to the bench by the screen and Doris painting the music for me in flowing cloth and movement. It's been worth the trip for Martha and Doris and Bach. And the image of my dad a dancing, butt-smoking hero.

On the way back I mention I liked "Air" and Doris. Thaddeus says, "Yeah, don't you love those first few seconds of listening when your brain figures out what it's hearing? Pure waiting. No verbal or visual aids, just sound. In class you hear that and then move. That's bliss!"

I'm not sure what he means, but I say yeah. Now every time a song starts, my mind does that sorting thing—*Do I know this? Do I like this? What is this?*—and I decide that's what T. was talking about. Too bad he's a senior about to leave. Too bad he's gay. If he is. I don't know, but Lacey's sure—for what that's worth, since she didn't even go on the trip.

At one point during our ride Thaddeus asks everyone, "Are you rich? I'm doing a poll." They go, Nah. Not really. What do you mean rich? and Henry goes, "No, mon!" T. nudges me with his elbow and says, "All farmers are rich, eh?" His grandparents from Jamaica said so. Also, he read it in the *New York Times*.

I told him we have a lot of stuff. I was thinking of our house and barn and cows and equipment. But I told him we weren't exactly rich, or why would my mother be washing his toilet. As soon as I say that, I regret it, because with those words I'm plunged back down to earth.

16

AFTER A QUIET, ANTICLIMACTIC WEEKEND, ON MONDAY snow rules, closes all the schools. The radio announces all the names in our area from Barnard to Williamstown and says to stay off the roads unless absolutely necessary. Even the college postpones the few exams left before break. It's Mom's day to clean, but she says she'll go tomorrow. Dad's worried about Wayne, the milk-truck driver. "Liquid loads are the worst," he says. But I think he's also worried about our super-full bulk tank, which won't have room for tonight's milk if ol' Wayne can't ride the drifts.

But in my own homeschool it's business as usual. Never closed—or should I say never open? I'm stuck, as usual. What will I learn today, heh heh? That the hydraulic cables on our bucket loader allow in moisture that freezes, which is why Dad can't clear the driveway and barnyard. He's scraping much more slowly with a blade instead. He's frosted with white every time I see him, his glasses iced up. We keep the cows in till he can scrape a place for them to walk outside.

What else? The snow shovel works better than the grain shovel for snow (duh!), but when I let Mom use the snow shovel my back feels stronger. We shovel a path from the house to the driveway and a longer path to the barn; we clear in front of the mailbox; we even shovel a path for the cats and for Waldo to favorite pooping spots up near the orchard. The snow is fluffy and we shovel, shovel, shovel.

Clay roars over on his "sled" early for afternoon chores: "No school! Need help?" Mom hands him the snow rake for the porch roof. We brush off the car, the truck, the porches, the front steps again, a path to the chicken house. I ask Clay if he remembers the Cat in the Hat cleaning up the snow with magic. "Sort of," he says. "Shoveling's okay." He's very talkative, for him. He starts to roll balls for a snowman, so I help and give it two heads and run inside to get two of Dad's feed caps. I'm clomping snow into the mudroom and I'm rushing, out of breath, having fun I guess. But then I think: *Cat in the Hat*? Is that my frame of literary reference for the day? I have to get out of here. Mom heads to the barn humming "Away in a Manger" off-key. That's art on this humdrum farm.

Then again, there's the snow! Powerful piles of cold white cover, bury, shape my shoveling shoulders, everyone's schedules. Snow defeats our machines, inspires song even in the tone-deaf, and sculpture in the farmhands. Snow. I eat it, throw it just shy of Mom's head, nick Clay on the knee with it.

While I'm lying in a drift, flapping an angel, Clay washes my face. The cold is unworldly. Almost hot. Specks fly everywhere in the white air. Blinking, glinting air. Ursula said the MS makes the edges of everything vibrate and dance. Is this what she means, this shimmering? Resculpting my home, farm, school, who does all this? God and us, even Clay, artists all. And there goes Whisper trotting lightly, not wanting to touch the snow, down his shoveled run to poop on this. He's the punk, the rebel, the installation maker. I guess I'm the romantic. Mom is Our Lady of the Snows. Her distant gaze is here today, blocked close, snowed in, humming away.

We do chores together in the stable, taking our time, warming our hands on the cows' flanks.

This is what I learned today. Snow rules, keeps us home. Snow, the general, commands, and cheerier than usual we obey.

After dinner, I read. Does everyone already know that both *The Giver* and "The Dead" have characters named Lily and Gabriel? And that snow plays a part in each? Duh. I need a teacher.

Then Lacey calls to tell me she's bored.

"I tanned today," she says. "My dad's taking us to Costa Rica for Christmas and I want to be ready. I'm so white it's disgusting."

I don't really know what to say. I think when I'm away from her that I should forgive and forget. Then she talks and I question if we're from the same planet. "I thought tanning was dangerous?" I say.

"Not really," she says. "It feels great and keeps S.A.D. away. Your mother should tan."

"I'll suggest that," I say, thinking how disconnected she is from the reality of my family.

There's a pause; then she asks what I'm doing. When I say I'm reading "The Dead," she goes, "Oh, great. Happy happy joy joy." I tell her no, it's good and not depressing, and she says, "Read me some."

I pick a line of Lily's, the maid, that I thought was funny. *The men that is now is all palaver and what they can get out of you.* Palaver, I tell her—I looked it up—means *talk to beguile.* "Funny word, huh?" I say.

No response. I'm feeling that disconnect again when out of the blue she asks, "Are you still a virgin?"

Which pisses me off, so I say, "Why, no, funny you should ask. I met this amazing guy in our mailbox. And every night we meet in the haymow and make passionate love on the nice soft hay, and the cats bring us rats for breakfast."

"Okay, I'm sorry. I just mean, well, someday you won't be, but just don't do it around here. Everyone here knows everything. Small towns are so pathetic. I gotta go. Later."

"Wait, what are you saying?" I ask. She's hung up. Rude.

What does she know, I wonder, about what I want? And what do I know about her? I know she had a thing with Ben Toulaine, but now I don't even know who she's hanging out with. If I were in school I'd know. Well, maybe not. We were in different classes.

I don't think we would be friends if it weren't for dance, and even there I don't think we look at dance the same way. It's not like we're soulmates, just bonded by circumstance.

In grade school all the kids were more or less friends, even if you had a rough family or were rich or something. I guess the teachers kept everything equal. Or little kids just don't care, not even about who's smart or dumb, as long as you're not mean or really weird, hiding under desks or crying a lot or smelling like pee.

But in high school everything matters. It's like everybody wants to be in a club made up of their own clones. Or they want to be clones of the most popular kids. Boring. Maybe I'm glad to have a break from that. But I won't tell Mom.

Last year there were these speakers, FDR and Eleanor Roosevelt "re-enactors." Sort of interesting from a physical point of view: him looking dignified in a wheelchair, her standing tall but made up to look ugly even though you could tell the actress wasn't. But I couldn't focus on what they were talking about because this girl in front of me was combing her hair the whole time with her fingers. I know her face, not her name. Her face is only so-so, but her hair is hypnotic, lustrous, light, long, full, like a shampoo ad. The speakers said, Questions? I wanted to know if they ever danced together. Did he dance before the wheelchair? I thought if she danced she would dance like Isadora, definitely not a ballet body, but maybe a grand waltzer, or a jitterbugger, or a clogger. Where did that leave him? Watching? Wheeling? Too bad. But of course I was guessing about the actress, not the real Eleanor. Were the actors married to each other? If they said, I never heard. I was watching the hair model. I didn't ask any questions at all.

I know—sigh—that Mom's right when she says school's not the greatest learning environment. The question is, as compared to what?

17

DAD CONTINUES HIS MISSION TO NORMALIZE, MODERNIZE farm life a bit. That is, to make more money. Here are his ideas as I understand them from the articles all over the kitchen and from every conversation he has with milk-truck drivers, grain dealers, the breeder, the vet, the tester, the inspector, his friend Pete, the mailman, and every other ear he can corner. On this subject he's chatty.

1. Go robotic and expand to 400 cows.

2. Go organic and get $25 cwt for milk.

3. Diversify. (He's talking llamas for taking tourists on hikes and for selling their wool? hair? and maybe do a corn maze and grow pick-your-own blueberries in the meadow by the pines, where the soil is most acidic.)

4. Develop part of the farm into house lots. (He says the governor's trying to make that easier.)

5. Produce value-added products like cheese and yogurt.

We discuss these at dinner. Dad's really interested only in #1. I vote for #2, even though I don't want to vote at all because that might implicate me in the farm's future, and Mom says they all sound like more work than what she's already got and what's wrong with the way things are, anyway? Go, Mom! Claim that wet-blanket award for the twentieth straight year!

Grampa says, "To earthly man his way does not belong.

It does not belong to man who is walking even to direct his step. Jeremiah 10:23." Spiritual wet blanket.

Mom interrupts the conversation to tell me it's my turn to do dishes. I don't mind doing dishes at night because I can play music. Dad has to wait to hear a game till I'm done. My favorite CD is Chopin's *Nocturnes*. Whisper squints when it's on, as if he were in pain. Waldo could care less and sleeps near Dad, who sleeps in the brown chair. But out flows Chopin and here's Whisper, summoned and disturbed, sitting in the middle of the kitchen, squeezing his eyes. *Too sad, too sad*, he's complaining. I tell him to go away. I wait for the magic. As I swish water in a pot, sadness churns into something else. The music pricks my heart and then dissolves into water or air and comes out through my fingertips, my throat, my toes, and I have to dance, waltzing, at the sink, washing and sloshing all the same. Movement so sweet, subtle, sensuous. Not every night, but when I'm in the mood and not too tired from stuff.

Tonight my feet hurt from my teach-yourself-pointe in the new shoes I bought with my own money. I think how they don't usually hurt in class. Nothing does. Another magic. Ballet turns pain into beauty too. Therefore ballet must be music.

When the CD ends I hear Dad snoring and the creak of the medicine cabinet in the bathroom. I bet Mom has a headache or her back is hurting. She was squinting during dinner. I thought it was the money discussion. But we have lots of treated cows, two with stepped-on teats. Mom and

Dad should listen to the music, better music, not just Fred Eaglesmith or about sexy tractors. They need better magic. Everyone says it is so beautiful here, but maybe farming turns beauty into pain. Is it black magic? Is that what adult life does? Beauty into pain? That sucks.

18

I NEED TO SAY ONE MORE THING ABOUT MONEY. TONIGHT I was cooking, and just when I'd put a pot of water on to boil for spaghetti, the phone rang.

"May I speak to Mrs. Snow?"

She was in the barn. "Speaking," I said.

"This is M.A.D.D."

Later, "This is Special Olympics. Thank you for your recent contribution."

"This is the Cancer Society."

No joke. It was an evening of causes. She's on all the lists. Apparently she's a Giver. Am I? I contemplate writing all these checks. I know the amount of the milk check. I know the grain bill, electric, vet, fuel, etc., because of my super-cool math project. I know there's no money for giving away. She says ten dollars each, we have that. And why must I buy my own pointe shoes? She's a mass of contradictions: stingy to me, magnanimous to strangers. Ugly to me, "beautiful wife" to Dad. And never does he get a happy smile in return, just a sad one. Still he keeps on … Is my mother beautiful because she is sad? How can he bear the pain of her? Is he completely insensitive? Or is he just too tired to see what's before his nose?

I want only radiant, happy beauty. No lines or etched rivulets for tears in my cheeks. I've read that movie stars use fake tears to cause their eyes to sparkle. I *know* there's another juice than tears for giving glint and the dazzle of jewel-like eyes. Happiness can be liquid. Like dance. I'm just not quite there yet.

19

I'M LOOKING AT THE CHRISTMAS CACTUS IN MY ROOM, from Dad—gorgeous in full red bloom. The flowers are just starting to curl and die. Now what do I do? He also gave me insulated coveralls from Wearguard with "Kit" on the pocket. Finally I fit into adult sizes and don't have to wear kids' snowsuits to keep warm. Clothes are easier to take care of than plants. This cactus has all these arms reaching out, rubbery soft but with jabbers. *Help/Go Away*, it seems to say. I'll water it when I remember, but I don't think it needs much. Dad doesn't know. He says it's supposed to bloom every Christmas and he smiles as if to say it's just the neatest thing he found for me, like he invented it or something. Mom doesn't believe in indoor plants any more than she believes in interior decorating of other kinds. For her, the world's out that window. She once said that bringing soil in, in *pots*, is as pointless as carpeting the cornfield would be. Even when I used to pick flowers for her, dandelions, daisies, clover, if *I* didn't put them in water, she always let them die, little wilty handfuls.

But I love flowers! Inside, outside, in my hair, in a vase, in a field, everywhere. I do, I love them, da-dee-dee, I'll tend that cactus, yes sirree!

What did Mom give me? Maybe she did the overalls (it said "From Santa" on them—cute). Socks and ridiculous underwear from Penney's. I sewed her an apron and

Dad a vest and Grampa a pillow, also a matching pillow for Waldo and two catnip mice for Whisper using nip dried from Grammy's overgrown garden. G.W. thanked me and gave me a kiss. He says Witnesses don't do Christmas, but he gave me a pretty scarf of Grammy's.

I may be outgrowing Christmas, I guess, because I yawned through Mass and during chores could no longer imagine that a baby in the manger of any barn would be more than a monumental pain in the butt.

Oh, Lacey, celebrating her sixteenth birthday on vacation in Costa Rica, sent me a card and *The Notebook*, which I read all afternoon and which depressed me no end. Also, Mom and Dad were napping all afternoon with their door closed, which was also depressing.

I had no energy to imagine Timmy or what he might get or the games we might play.

Clay, of course, had the day off, but he came in the evening anyway with cookies from his mother and also to milk because he was bored, since it's forty degrees, the snow's melted, and all he got was the snowmobile gloves, helmet, and Snow Travelers pass he wanted. Says he played Mortal Combat with his brother all day. Dad says we should all move to Canada for their milk quota system and better snow. Global warming, I say, and you don't believe me.

My body has started to crave a barre. I stretch some in my room, in the kitchen. It's never enough. I tweak my knee. I never get hurt in class. The days grind by. I feel like I'm waiting for something to happen. When I see "Dancers" in Help Wanted I'm tempted to apply.

Just before New Year's Lacey calls to invite me to her party. I'm tired of being mad, so it's a relief to hear from her. She says Costa Rica was great, blah blah blah, she went surfing, next year I should come with her. I tell her I want to learn to surf. She says, "Ask, girl, and you shall receive." She sounds like Grampa! I tell her I'm stir-crazy and dying to dance. She says I have to get out more. She says every girl's nightmare is to be home all day with her mother. She says that even if you basically think your mother is okay, every day is excessive. Excessive. Relentless. This closeness is stifling, senseless. I say yeah, a girl shouldn't have to smell her mother in the bathroom, you know? I mean, I'm fifteen, fully housetrained; I can cook, I can sew, grow a garden, clean house, drive a car, a truck, a tractor. I have other talents too. Mom's job is done. I'm done, grown, finished. Isn't it time for me to fly the coop? All animals leave their mothers. It's nature's way. God's plan and all that. It's my turn. If not today, damn soon.

Lacey agrees, lets me rant. It feels good to talk. I tell her I'm thinking of applying for a job as a dancer, but Lacey says you have to be eighteen to do those parties and they check really carefully.

20

New Year's Eve, Eleanor has a huge heifer right before milking. I suggest Janus for the name. Janus, from Latin, looking forward, looking back. Florence has a bull calf that I suggest calling Heretic, but of course we don't name bulls. I'm just in that kind of mood. Everything runs late. With the new calves, Eleanor down with milk fever, a broken link in the gutter-cleaner chain, and milking, I don't get out of the barn till nine. I'm hungry and tired.

I call Lacey to say I can't go to her party. She says, "Whoa, why can't you? Chores ran late? Chores do not rule the world." That's what *she* thinks. They clearly rule my house. I should resolve to take control of my life, she says. "Whose dream is the farm anyway?" she asks. No more should I be the good daughter of the dreams ol' Ma and Pa have. Now for *my* dreams, and for making them happen: tell them no chores *ever* on weekend nights.

I would not have been able to go to her party even without the chores, I tell her. Mom says she knows there'll be drinking.

Lacey says, "Sneak out. I'll pick you up in my car."

Her car. I say, "Maybe." But it seems too complicated. I tell her about Janus, and try to describe the perfectness of the two-faced name, looking forward, looking back, poised between places. What I mean is, are we balanced or are we stuck? I tell her Janus is our existential condition. I tell her

I think maybe Janus will become my E.D. 7 to show next summer.

Lacey interrupts. "Kit, stop. Aren't you a little old for that? I mean, it's so retro, isn't it, dressing in white, shampooing tails, pulling them around in a circle like Miss America or something? Do you even want to do that? You've got to stop getting sucked back in. Just come. I'll pick you up."

Easy for her to say.

I remember in seventh grade we had D.A.R.E. and Officer Everett described how we start off each day with a fully inflated balloon of happiness, self-esteem, etc. Then, he said, you come downstairs and before you even eat breakfast your big sister or brother says, "Yech, that zit looks worse than yesterday!" and your balloon deflates a little. Your mother says, "Clean the litter box! You always forget." *Pfft*—more air escapes. By the time you get through the bus ride, first classes, a pop quiz, lunch, you've got an empty balloon on your hands.

I don't know about the rest of D.A.R.E., but that little parable is true. It's like bloodletting, the way some people, Lacey and my mother *especialement*, can deflate my balloon and make me sag.

Exhausting! I just fall into bed. I don't even *want* to go to the party. I just want to dance or sleep.

21

Next day, I finally put my foot down and stay home from church. Whoopee. Maybe the priest will assume I was out partying like a normal teenager. I do my favorite stretches and all the barre exercises I can remember. I avoid the overloaded cookie platter and start to feel a little better. But then for history I read about the Donner Party, which takes away all appetite.

In the afternoon Lacey calls to say the party sucked but there's a vegetarian potluck at Greensbrook Unitarian Church to celebrate the Great American Meat-Out. Meat makes me think of the Donner Party. I tell Lacey to consider this: twenty families following jerk-o Langford Hawkins's promises of a shortcut to California. They vote, oh sure, but the women can't vote, and what happens? They get trapped and end up eating each other while stuck in a brutal winter. And they all die anyway.

Lacey says that wouldn't have happened if they'd listened to the women, and I say, well, women can vote now and the world's still a mess, and she says at least we're not eating each other.

She's got me there. Not a cannibal in our whole acquaintance, at least not that we know of.

I tell her I don't feel like going to the potluck, even though she says Ursula usually goes. Ursula! But what if Ursula wasn't there and I had to listen to Lacey all evening?

Lacey is less and less my idea of the perfect pal.

And Mom, my dear Mom, has made roast beef and Yorkshire pudding, Grampa's favorite, for New Year's, not even trying to be PC. She is so clueless. I tell her it's the Great American Meat-Out. She says I'm welcome to go. Dad adds, "Sure, bring 'em a bale of hay for dessert." Grampa chuckles. I consider leaving them laughing.

I mention the Donner Party, wondering if they know about it. Grampa goes, "Donkey Party?" and Mom goes, "Another party? We have to vaccinate this weekend." Not *that* kind of party, I say, and I briefly tell the tale. "Oh," she says, "how sad." She's often clueless, but she has some common sense. She'd never have followed Langford Hawkins. Too stubborn. The food smells good, so I eat some, sighing like a dying balloon. I hate that I'm spineless to resist.

Another pathetic thing: her rooster, Thunderbird, is in a cage in the corner of the kitchen. I guess all roosters are known for huge, scary, even scaly, knobby feet with majorly sharp, hooked talons. But T-bird's are off the scale (no pun intended) for sharpness and ugliness. Actually, scale is what has turned his feet from healthy yellow to gray/white this winter and added layers of ridges and lumps. Scale = little bugs. Sweet. He's in for the night because it's suddenly ten below and low temps bother his feet excessively. If he doesn't improve and if the weather stays cold, Dad will end T-bird's misery and Mom will mope and pluck at the same time. So, not only do we eat meat on the night of the Meat-Out, we let future dinners come to *watch* us eat dinner!

I wish I could say now that Thunderbird wouldn't hurt a flea in spite of his foul (!) appearance, but alas, 'twouldn't be true. Those poor hens get pinned every day with those claws while Thunderbird does his mindless male thing. Grampa calls it "treading on 'em." I've seen roosters do a little dance around a hen to get them in the mood. In most, the dancing's been bred out of them. Shame. Thunderbird is not a dancer, just a pouncer. I am so glad I'm not a chicken. So glad, *so* glad! Not a hen and certainly not T-bird.

Humans have their faults, I know. But I just don't see people acting that way. They are a cut above chickens. Then again, consider the Donner Party. Short on chicken bones, maybe they should have tried divination by other bones to find their way out before everyone was dead.

PART TWO

1

FINALLY! THE SUBS ARE HERE! LUIS AND CLARA COLL AND baby Lola. When we arrive for class they are simply there occupying the studio, no introduction or *grande* entrance. Luis just says, "Come in, come in, to the barre, sweatshirts off, please, let's see what we have here."

I love the purity of the encounter, and his class. Strictly ballet. All and only ballet. He says ballet is the most royal of dance. In a black T-shirt and tights his body looks royal, exquisite. Lean, carved muscles look powerful as coiled rope, still, waiting to whip into action. Hers too. They make me think of high-class horses. Next to them Ursula's body would seem more like a workhorse, handsome also, but rougher-cut. Of course, she isn't around for comparison. They are staying at her house, apparently, but I haven't seen her in a month. I am so glad her place is finally filled. Every time I've been in the studio her absence has left me feeling hollow. Classes have been fun games, like charades, not the real thing.

Luis smiles at us; Clara, thin and blond, seems more remote. Dressed in black warm-ups with a black fringed shawl, she sits cross-legged, her straight spine mirrored behind her. She watches without a word. The baby sleeps, a small bundle against her belly in a purple sling. Occasionally during class I'll spot a tiny fuzzy head covering most of a peeking breast.

I've never seen a baby nursing before. It's not like a calf at all, no slurping or head butting, just quiet and gentle and shocking all at once.

Luis asks each of us our name, although he seems to know Naheema and a few others. He repeats mine, "Kit," carefully and smiles at me. "Yes," he says, "Kit and Lacey, our younger ballerinas. Ursula told us about you." Everything is *we, our, us,* as though he and Clara are team-teaching. "We hold the arms so," "Please, again for us." As we do the barre exercises he says, "Show us your soul." Then he lifts his face and chest and looks magnificent, a cleaned-up, stripped-down modern Aragorn. (We rented *The Fellowship of the Ring* Saturday night.) Soul? Or body?

What does my soul look like? I feel incredibly blank when he says that. As if it were easy. As if I could decide to show it or not. Oh, I know he means express more—but maybe to him, being older, it's easy to show his soul, not a big deal. I wonder, do you know what you're asking? Okay, wait right there for about like five years while I find my soul; then I might or might not show it to you, Prince Aragorn. I'm thinking this while I'm doing this simple adagio. Mozart. Then he goes, "Ah, good, Kityana. Now you look alive. *Très bien.*"

He calls me Kityana. He gives me lots of corrections. I feel like a beginner, but I love the intensity. Lacey says after class, "This royal-'we' shit is excessive, don't you think, and what's with the Russky nickname?" I think all he said to her was, "Heel forward. Heel forward."

Two days later, Luis comes to class alone. The baby has a doctor's appointment. He hates to miss it, L. says. Each moment with a newborn, he says, holds a million changes. Growth is visible, exciting, he says. A young dancer can be like that, he says. Growing, changing, developing by the moment. Be alive and open as babies, he says.

Yes, yes, I feel that charge of excitement, of rebirth in his class.

My body feels so strong (also sore!) and alive. It's been so long since our classes had this degree of rigor. Not everyone feels this way. Now Lacey calls him His Highness. I hear Thaddeus murmur to Naheema on the stairs after class, "Be alive and open as a babe."

But I feel the rightness of his teaching in my bones. Divination by bones. Maybe, like Grammy, I have a gift. I feel it from Luis as he watches me.

Saturday is the contradance fundraiser for Ursula. Unfortunately, I'm there only briefly, since I got a ride with Lacey and she doesn't want to stay long. She has a date with someone, apparently, but doesn't want to talk about it. When we arrive she goes, "Oh goody, it's the Holy Family."

It happens in a whirl. I dance with him. Of course, at a contradance you dance with practically everyone at some point and he wasn't my partner or anything, but when he swung me around I felt in such good hands. I love to turn anyway and Ursula says I'm a natural turner. I love the breeze of air brushing my face, the excitement of breath gasped quickly.

His eyes hold mine as we spin. I think he sees inside my spirit. He squeezes my hand before I leave. "Good night, Kit," he says.

Clara comes over to me and Lacey as we put on our coats and says that Ursula had mentioned that we might be interested in babysitting sometime. "Her," Lacey blurts, "not me. No offense, but babies spook me." Also, I know she doesn't need the money.

2

Ms. Wiseman arrives Saturday morning with a huge grin, drops a load of books on the kitchen table, and says to Mom, "How are the cows doing?" as if they concern her. She went to school with Mom a hundred years ago and they're sort of friends, or friendly anyway. Maybe she did a project on cows sometime or maybe she grew up on a farm or something.

She gives Mom an hour of advice, although I don't know what makes her an expert on homeschooling, since she teaches in an actual school and her own kids are supersmart and go to places like Dartmouth. Mom keeps saying, "Kit, are you listening?" She tells Ms. W., "Kit's really her own teacher, you know?" Which I'm sure impresses Ms. W. with our level of organization. She says if I do a project and enter it at the high school science fair it counts as an "assessment tool." And that would be good if I ever want to get any credit for my year of Hard Time. My words, those last.

Anyway, after she's gone it's not hard to continue my interrupted research on "Bats and Their Importance to Farming"—"If farmers weren't batty there'd be no farms, and no farms equals no food." Period. A direct quote from the mathematical wizard also known as my dad. That's what he said when we were talking about my possible project and other trivial things at dinner. Notice: we never delve into things. Conversations are glib, as if everything were as simple as a few Dad or Grampa quips here and there.

"I have to do this scientifically," I tell them.

"Bats are good 'cause they're skeeter traps," Grampa says.

"Listen to this." I read from an extension flyer Ms. W. tucked into one of her books. "In Indiana, a colony of just one hundred fifty big brown bats, *eptesicus fuscus*, consumes sufficient cucumber beetles each summer to prevent egg laying that would produce thirty-three million of their rootworm larvae, another costly pest."

"Ooo, no bats, no pickles," Mom says.

"Or you'd have to spray those beetles to kingdom come," Grampa adds. I stare at him, kind of shocked he's taking the Kingdom's name in vain. They are making light of a subject I like, and it pisses me off.

I read on. "Loss of roosting habitats is causing more than half of the forty-five species of bats in the U.S. and Canada to be endangered. Caves are closing, forests are being cut, old buildings gentrified. And now their usefulness is threatened by White Nose Syndrome."

"They may be useful," Mom interrupts, "but they're still ugly and move funny. They don't fly right, like normal birds."

"God," I say, "they're not birds, they're mammals. Move funny? How they loop through the air up by the barn roof? They're beautiful. Remember that one in the house?"

She rolls her eyes. "No," she lies.

A few years ago Mom and I were shelling dry beans in the kitchen; Dad was in the barn, I guess, or at a fire department meeting, I don't remember, but anyway he was not around and neither were G.W. and Grammy or it wouldn't have been nearly so much fun.

First thing we see Whisper the Blob, lazy guy, go crazy. He streaks around the kitchen and takes this amazing Baryshnikov leap into the air. Think Nijinsky. Think Michael Jordan. Whoa, I want to applaud, but lines have gathered on Mama's brow. She hunkers down gripping crunchy beans by the handful and says, "Darn." I follow the line of Mom's glare and Whisper's acrobatics, and there, tucked between the molding above the door and the kitchen ceiling, hangs a quivering brown bat. Hanging upside down, just the way you'd expect. Whisper's teeth are chattering in that demented excitement song of his, and I bet the bat's are too. His wings are trembling anyway and so are the corners of Mom's mouth. A freaky trembly trio. All I can do is watch … and what drama!

Very slowly she goes to the wall behind the woodstove where a broom leans; she wraps both hands around the handle. Never lets her gaze leave the bat. She's terrified of the thing, I can tell. Through clenched teeth, she says, "Open the door."

Me, I think it's cute. Just like a puppet I have that Grammy Rose gave me.

"Don't hurt him," I say. "Don't let Whisper get him."

She swats at it suddenly with the broom; it rides the bristles for a second and then zigzags *zoop zoop* and out the door. Whisper follows in a flash before I can close the door, but it would have been a miracle if he'd caught it. He has trouble catching a cluster fly.

Back then I don't think I noticed my mother's affinity for brooms, for sweeping life and my desires out the door.

3

IN THE BARN I WATCH LITTLE DEBBIE SCRATCH HER
head with a rear hoof. She shifts to the standing legs so
smoothly, no wobble. That's balance.

On the walkway behind her I practice standing on one
leg in *relevé* and shifting weight to the other. Mom goes,
"Just milk, can you, you're making the cows nervous with
all that flailing around."

I was hardly flailing. She doesn't know balance when
she sees it. Does she even notice the cows, modeling perfect
physical poise? Chickens do it too when they rest on one leg,
the other tucked up. Context is everything. All the world is
not a stage around here. She apparently can't see the beauty
in balance any more than she can see beauty in bats.

But in class today Luis showed this beautiful blue fairy
costume of Clara's. The camisole seemed made of fine silk and
beads with delicate birdlike ribs. He said it doesn't fit her now,
after having Lola. But you see, he said, how petite you must be?
Tiny to lift, like air. No one in Ver-Mont is that small, he said
with a sad frown. He put the costume away with a flourish, poof,
like a magician. I saw Eveline roll her eyes at Naheema. Not
their style. E. is curvy and wears sarongs. Me, I like that little
costume. It makes me dream. I floated through class. I kept my
balance in the adagio by thinking of the camisole hugging my
ribs and of Marge, Mom's lone remaining Silkie, skinny legs,
one standing, one updrawn, perfectly centered.

"That's it, Kityana," Luis said.

That's it, Kityana, I think as I drive home with Mom after class in white-out snow.

"Where is the road?" Mom, gripping the wheel, says. "It's meant to clear; we'll see the wolf moon," and then she doesn't talk at all, which is preferable.

That's it, Kityana, I think as I practice behind Little Debbie in the barn and Mom accuses me of flailing.

And later, in my room, I scrape frost from the window to see the full moon breaking through dark clouds lighting the new snow. The wolf moon of January. I wish I liked the cold so I could walk out there; it is so beautiful, like a stage, like a set.

Luis does really look like Aragorn. I loved the movie. Loved those books. Of course I can't help liking him. Imagine Aragorn dancing the way he looks or the way he rides a horse—strong, powerful. A knight. A king. King of the night, he comes late and throws a snowball against this window. Everyone else is asleep; I can hear Dad snoring as I tiptoe downstairs. I put on my insulated coveralls but shouldn't have because Luis laughs when he sees me and draws me into his open furry coat and whispers, *So much clothes, Kityana? I would keep you warm*. His breath spreads heat from my ear to my toes, but I say, *Not here*, and take his hand and pull him away from the eyes of the house. We walk in the tractor tire tracks along the logging trail up the hill behind the barn and to the edge of the woods. The moon balances, a perfect O on the rim of the east ridge.

We watch it swell. *The world is ours*, he whispers into my lips. And we kiss until even kisses can't keep out the cold and we have to run, fast but silent sylphs, to the barn. The cows breathe sweet and steamy, and we warm our hands laid across Sweetpea's back, tips touching. Finally he says, *I have to go*, leans in to kiss me once, and lays his fingers against my cheek. I close my eyes. He doesn't want me to walk way down the hill to where he's left his car, but I wait by the barn till he's out of the spotlight of the moon.

In my room now I love the night, I love the cold. I would love it if that really happened.

Classes have become more than dance. They are exciting, almost breathless. I start bringing him eggs from our hens, give them to him and Clara after class. He is ecstatic, his smile radiant.

Then, outside in the dusky cold, when Mom sees someone (it's Luis!) peering under the hood of his car, she offers to help. She hauls out cables and we get his Honda going, me at our wheel, Luis at his, Mom with her red, gloveless hands working the cables. Mom, breath spewing, tells him he probably needs a new battery. I'm partly mortified and partly thrilled by the excuse to talk to him, so I hop out to introduce them.

Back in our car Mom says, "I knew who that was. Hey, were those our eggs on the back seat near the baby? Don't give them away, Kit. We eat them or sell them. You know our numbers are down ever since the fox."

"You always gave them to Ursula," I say.

"Yeah, well."

I swear she cannot touch anything in my life without wrecking it.

4

LUIS TOUCHES ME IN CLASS. TRULY. MY FOOT STILL SINGS
as though he imparted life with his hand. The firm, warm
grip urging my heel forward.

As class ends he says, "Kit, can we see you for a
minute?" and waves me to the front of the studio, where
Clara sits with Lola. He tells me that in March there's an
audition for L'Académie des Arts in Montreal. He says it
would be an absolutely perfect match for me. He and Clara
were guest artists there two years ago and they totally loved
it. The students adored them and the director begged them
to stay, but of course they couldn't because of their performance schedule.

Luis says it's got everything I need and can't get here:
beautiful studios, great teachers, ballet, modern, character,
jazz, a fitness center, and an adorable performance space.
Most importantly, Luis says that throughout, emanating
from every hallway, is *respect* for dance, music, drama, and
all the arts. And the academics are good too.

"You here in Vermont," Clara murmurs as she lifts
Lola to her shoulder and rises swiftly, "yes, the air is fresh,
but you are so stunted. No art, no money for art, no love
for art."

Yes, yes, I agree. It's true. *C'est vrai.* This is so amazing,
them thinking I could actually move forward, be what I
want to be. I don't know what to say. This is happiness.

Luis says, "So, talk it over with your parents. It will be hard work, but we'll help you prepare."

I'm ecstatic. I glide through the rest of the afternoon. I scarcely remember doing chores, thinking instead of the whole world away from here—exciting, purposeful, connected with people and great ideas. In the kitchen, filling a pot with water, I look out Mom's window and no longer wonder why she's depressed and depressing. It's pretty out there—sure it's pretty. The elm is a stark bouquet of branches, the snow-covered fields are like clouds on earth. Sunset lighting the sky is purplish rose all the way to the rolling hills of Hogback. But empty. Boring. "Winter on the Farm." Unremitting. Been here, done this. A gang of crows crowds into the elm, bickering. A lone graceful hawk bursts from the branches and glides away into the sugar woods with the crows flapping and yakking in pursuit. Poor hawk. So beautiful, attacked by jerks.

Mom looks up from chopping onions. "Must be that Cooper's hawk been troubling the chickens."

Even eating here is a chore. Frozen broccoli again, potatoes, applesauce, fried onions, and chops from a pig Clay's mom raised named Silver. Gag! I want more than this.

I broach the sensitive subject at supper. "Luis says there's this school in Montreal where he and Clara taught. A school that would be perfect for me. Great academics and dance together in the same place." I hold my breath.

"You don't need to think about college yet," Mom says.

"No, no, no—for now! It's a high school," I say. But her wording, *You don't need to think*, rattles me. She's going to ruin this.

Mom says, "Oh, not now. You're too young. And you're needed here. That's the deal: eighteen years in the nest, then fly away if you want."

"The deal? What deal?" I try to control my voice. I look to Dad for help.

He shrugs. "You're awful young to go away. But maybe"—he looks at Mom—"it's time for her to go back to Greensbrook."

What! As if I'm not there, he's talking now about my old high school! I'm no longer timidly praying. "You're changing the subject. I want this. It's called Academy of the Arts. The audition is in March." Their faces are frowning, both looking at the damn pork chops. "If I were a boy, you'd let me go," I say.

"To ballet school?" Mom looks up and actually smiles.

"God, you think that's funny, it just shows how narrow your mind is."

I get up to leave.

Mom's telling Dad, "Say something."

Dad says, "I'm thinking."

I'm thinking too, and what I'm thinking is, *I'm going in March.*

5

LUIS SAYS I MUST SEE THE NEW SCULPTURE EXHIBIT AT the college gallery called "Rodin: In His Own Words."

"Amazing to find it here," he says as he coaches me after class on *pas de bras*. "Nice strong arms," he says.

I go alone while I wait for Mom to finish cleaning. Amazing. I feel *The Falling Man and the Crouching Woman* and *Paolo and Francesca* in my gut. I want to pet the figures like animals, caress them with my hands. On the gallery walls are cards with Rodin's words. One says he "endeavored to express the inner feelings by the mobility of the muscles." Exactly! Just like dance!

I drift from one piece to the next. His words speak straight to me: "One does well only what one does daily." I know that. Practice, practice, practice. And this about *Tragic Muse*: "The great artist, and by this I mean the poet as well as the painter and the sculptor, finds even in suffering, in the death of loved ones, in the treachery of friends, something which fills him with a voluptuous though tragic admiration." See, it's that thing about sadness becoming beautiful. I've thought the thoughts of an artist.

When you leave the exhibit you can take a postcard (if you're a student; otherwise they cost three bucks each! I guess it pays to be a student) of *The Thinker*. A souvenir. I have it on the wall by my bed. *I've* been thinking. Hee-hee-hee.

Imagine taking his pose. Sit nude on a rock, a big, black, craggy rock. Rest your left forearm on your left knee and lean forward till your right elbow rests also on your left quad just above the knee. Your chin is supported by the back of your right hand, pointing in toward your right shoulder like a bird's beak.

Your foot soles are braced against the rock, which is chiseled away to give you a level seat. Left foot slightly higher than the right so left thigh is slightly higher, taking all that weight of both arms, inclined torso, chin, head. Comfortable? No way.

Why doesn't he lean on the right leg? I would.

But I guess it wouldn't be pretty. The Thinker is a spiral, a luscious, twisting muscle man. And thought is movement, not a pose. Hmm ...

I think dance is more truthful than stone or clay or bronze. Anyway, I think the Thinker should put both arms on the right knee. Still a spiral but much more comfortable. Maybe to Rodin thought *was* uncomfortable. That would make sense. The Thinker is only one form from these huge doors called *The Gates of Hell*. Maybe Rodin believed thinking leads to hell. Heck, I don't know what the guy was thinking. He just loved the feel of bodies. You sure can tell that.

On the bulletin board outside the art building, scrawled across multiple flyers announcing a Valentine's Day dance, are these words: "Can You Dance When There's a War On?" The answer of course is yes. We do, every class. If I were a senior, that would be my senior project, my grand *chef d'oeuvre*. Trace great dancers and dances and their relation to war. At least I think yes would be the answer.

We are in a bubble here, I know it. Montreal will be more real.

Sometimes I feel unreal. Even my name seems flimsy. Kit. Kitty. My name is so cutesy, so little and wee, I might as well be a doll or a pet. Come to think of it, Waldo and Whisper have better names than that.

I love that Luis calls me Kityana, even though Thaddeus told me it sounds like Kitana, a character in Mortal Combat, the video game.

6

I'VE BABYSAT FOR A LOT OF KIDS, BUT THIS IS THE FIRST time for Lola; she is the sweetest baby, with a tiny soft head; she's really good and I love giving her a bottle. Love it. After she's settled in her crib I love wandering around their tiny apartment in the back of Ursula's house and seeing their stuff. Mostly baby stuff, and piles of clothes, and a huge futon with a nest of disheveled blankets. Everything smells like baby powder. Their kitchen cupboard holds twelve kinds of tea, of which I sample Wild Berry Zinger; in their refrigerator are five chocolate bars, all dark, different brands, that I don't dare open.

It's hard to imagine Clara eating them. She's always so cool and formal. Not sweet. No chitchat. She sort of scares me. Before they left for dinner—their "first date," Luis said, "since Lola was born"—Clara stood at the door pulling on thin black gloves. "I wrote down the restaurant number, but unfortunately my cell doesn't work around here," she said to me. "Are you sure you're up to this? Lola may cry."

"Sure." I smiled, wanting her to smile back, but she didn't, so I added, "I can always get Ursula if there's a problem."

"Not home. She went to a doctor in Boston." Now Clara looked grim.

"Come, come, come!" Luis put his arm around her, ushering her out as he opened the door. "Kityana has our number. She'll be fine."

I was about to say, Well, I can always call my mother, but they were gone.

Clara never talks much. In class she seems slightly distracted and totally involved with Lola or with her own stretching. The word "aloof" comes to mind. She has taught the itty-bitty pointe classes at the end of Luis's regular classes, but they are basic, basic, basic, as though she thinks we are so bad we can't learn anything hard. She says she is surprised we are not further along, but she agrees with Ursula that we can't do more if we don't dance every day. Besides, she says, by college it's really too late to accomplish much. She's invited two twelve-year-olds from the kiddie class that I never took to join us, which makes me feel strange. Odd man out. I should be so much further ahead at my age, but then again I'm not as hopeless as the college kids, who don't really care anyway. She says they want exercise and fun and an easy credit. She says that to me and Lacey, to the two twelve-year-olds, and to Naheema, who sometimes takes the class. Well, not *you*, she says to N., but I see N. shut down. Her loyalties are clear, but I don't see how she can deny the truth of what Clara says. Thaddeus and Henry joke around with Luis, but they don't always heed his corrections. Luis says I'm the most teachable of the lot.

One day after class I straight-out ask Clara if it's too late for me. She's putting away CDs and wrapping her own gorgeously broken-in Grishkos in their ribbons. She's humming to herself but stops and looks at me.

"How old are you?" She peers at me as though she's never seen me before.

"Fifteen," I say, wanting for just that moment to be a prodigy of ten or eleven. "But I practice every day."

She smiles and rolls her eyes. "Oh, yes, Luis says in your barn or something. And now you want to go to L'Académie. That's good. They have all kinds of dance, not just ballet. But to get in you need ballet. You are behind the fifteen-year-olds there, but who knows? Work hard. That world is very competitive. You must be realistic."

Her words feel like a punch in the stomach. *Must.* That sounds like my mother.

Luckily, Luis glides in just then, holding Lola lightly like a doll along one arm. I touch her little hand and let her tiny fingers curl around my long pointer.

"Tsk, no, don't discourage her," Luis says to Clara. He seems annoyed. To me he says, "You will stand out because of your quality of movement, your musicality, your love of dancing, and"—here he smiles—"the red hair. But Clara is right about the competition. So many girls want to be bal-lerinas. So few will be. You have to work harder and"—now he gestures to the room—"you have to go where you can get the best training. Not here, old creaky studio, bad floor, and not in a barn either." He smiles again, but sadly this time.

Clara takes over the gurgling, flapping Lola, who is starting to whimper, and says, "Time to go. Luis, can you get the bag?" She heads out; he touches my shoulder and follows.

I say I'll get the lights, but they don't hear. I stay on for a few minutes, just me alone in the studio that looks shabby to me now, but precious, with the magical mirror reflecting my true self. I kick my shoes off and pull tall, looking good even in jeans and a poofy coat. I spring into action like a deer, a gazelle, running and leaping and slipping in my socks around that sacred space. The floorboards give their creaky applause. I land in a low lunge, bow forward, and give the floor a kiss.

They return from their "date" before midnight. Luis is driving me home and we take the long way, by way of Mount Ida Road, because Jackrabbit Road is completely muddified from the global-warming thaw we're having. We're going along in a foggy mist and he says, "I hope you don't mind if I smoke. It's been a long day," and reaches into his pocket. Before I say anything, he turns to look at me. "Okay if I smoke?"

I say something like "Mm-hmm." I mean, it's his car.

I do hate smoke, but I'm thinking that maybe smoking isn't that bad for you if you exercise a lot, like Luis. And Dad smokes. Maybe all my men will be smokers.

I can't believe I thought that! I tell him, "My dad smokes."

"Hmm," says Luis as he cracks his window and sends a plume that way. I watch his lips. "Want one?" he says. His eyes catch the light of a car passing. He looks mysterious, or mean. Is he teasing me?

"No," I say. "I tell my dad it's bad for him. Lola will probably tell you."

Luis laughs. "Good girl." Now he's smiling, looking amused and happy. I make him happy. "It's a very bad habit." He's still smiling. "Clara has stopped and I'm all alone. Poor me. All alone." He sighs, hugely, and looks suddenly sad in a smoke cloud.

"Well," I say, "you could stop too. Or come smoke on our porch with my dad." Brilliant me, I've come up with two ways for him not to be alone. Not that he's asking me for any.

He laughs like I'm hilarious. "Oh, little Kityana, you crack me up. Enough about my foul habit."

He throws the butt out the window. I hate that usually, those flying sparks, I don't know why, but tonight they break the dark with a happy flash. He drives squinting into the fog for a minute. I try to think of something to say.

"Tell me about you, Kit, one new thing, one secret of yours. Just between us. What is most … unusual about you?"

He asks me this, I swear to God. I am not making this up. It's like he read my mind, knew I wanted to say something, and sent just the right question to help me out. He does this when he's teaching too, draws you out. *Lift the knee, Kityana, and now extend the leg to the sky.*

It's late; the car is dark and slow, a little foggy on the inside from smoke and very foggy outside. I don't see how he can drive. I see only white swirls in the headlights. We seem the only ones awake in town. Maybe we're the only ones in the world in our traveling box. Like Explorers, space travelers, the Next Generation, the Same Generation.

I say, "I like my body."

I feel as though I've jumped off Rainbow Cliffs at the river, same stupid breathless plunge. A shiver goes through me. Did I really say that? I had to because it really is my secret, and the most unusual thing I could think of. I mean, Lacey and all the girls I know hate their boobs or their stomachs, or their feet or their eyebrows, and I just don't. Maybe because dancing makes me feel so good I just assume it must look okay, or maybe because I spend so much time outside and in a barn where there's no mirror and no one cares about looks, except the looks of the cows or the corn. I feel like my body is a tool for doing things, and it works. I'm a tuned instrument, like Ursula always told us to be—a sharp knife, a good shovel, a tied knot, a packed snowball. Something useful, full of energy, trimmed of excess. I know it's weird and conceited-sounding and almost un-American.

I don't tell *him* all that, but get this: Luis leans to me and whispers like smoke, "I know, Kityana. That's no secret. That's the way you dance. Movement never lies."

My heart thumps, pounding so hard it almost pumps through my skin; when Luis reaches for my hand, palm up, I kinda slap his. Idiot, idiot, I'm going gimme five, and he, like silk, takes my fingers and pulls them to his mouth and, yes, kisses them. I kid you not.

"Here's my mailbox," I say. Idiot!

He lets go of my hand to turn the wheel with both of his. He has to concentrate on driving so as not to get stuck in ruts; we are quiet the rest of the way. Him peering straight ahead, me feeling my heart thump all over my head, my chest, my gut, my fingertips. I can't think. I breathe and pound and just sit there breathing and pounding away. What was that he said? *Movement never lies, movement never lies.*

At my house he goes, "No Daddy smoking on the porch. Too late. Very late. Go to sleep. Sleep well. Thank you, Kityana. Lola thanks you."

I guess I say bye. He turns the car around and bumps his way back up the driveway to the road. His headlights hardly dent the fog. The porch steps are icy, but the air is mild. The first skunk smell of the season lingers nearby.

As I shut the kitchen door behind me I hear Mom's voice from upstairs. "Kit, that you?"

I slide off my boots, hang my coat, and switch off the light before going to the bottom of the stairs and hissing, "Yes." She'll wake Dad if she hasn't already, she'll ruin the spell.

"See you in the morning," she says.

I go to the bathroom, then lie in bed with my fingers brushing my cheek till Whisper jumps aboard, invading my space with little head butts demanding *pet me pet me pet me.*

THE KITCHEN IS SUNNY NEXT MORNING AFTER BREAKFAST.
I sit near the stove, trying to concentrate on bats. I can
still feel my heart beating, the warm tenderness of his lips
and breath touching my fingers. I bring them to my cheek.
Whisper snoozes beside me, purring. Grampa turns the pages
of the newspaper. Waldo's tail thumps the floor. Mom sloshes
dishwater, flicks on the CD player. Dad's making z's upstairs.

I finger my bookmark, the valentine from Lacey. It says
Follow your bliss, shows a picture of a cat crouched under a
bush watching birds at a feeder. Sick. But what is my bliss?
What I feel now? This bubbling under my skin? I want to be
free and wild, not one of the domesticated animals in our
family herd. Freedom, art, passion. Not this kitchen cozi-
ness.

Could I survive in the wildness of the woods? Or in
the civilization of a city? Where do I belong? In that car last
night, in my skin now, in the studio later.

Mom's valentine from Dad stands on the windowsill
in front of her. It's a picture of a woman sweeping in a sunlit
barn of Jerseys with a quote from Kahlil Gibran: *Work is
love made visible.* Everything in Mom's life is a chore.

*This must be love because I feel so good, no pain, no
sorrows, no tears* ... Mom's tape of some musical plays while
she does dishes. Wouldn't she be surprised to hear that it
applies to me?

Mom says, out of the blue, "Kit, the Tractor Safety course at the extension service starts next week."

I know she wants desperately for me to do this. She's mentioned it a hundred times. It seems stupid, but thinking of Timmy and Roland I say, "Okay."

"It meets on dance nights, Monday, Wednesday, four to six. But only for two weeks."

Couldn't have been better designed to screw up my life. I say, "Absolutely not."

8

Luis isn't ordinary L-o-u-i-s. It's L-u-i-s. Luis, Luis, Luis, Luis. The name, even so many repetitions of it, cannot begin to express his power as a dancer. He is music, a drum pulsing deeply, a guitar vibrating intensely string by string. He is sharp; he is fluid. He is so incredibly strong. Oh, God. He is a god. With a face. Almond-shaped, cocoa-colored eyes with arching brows and lashes as long as this girl Melanie's false ones from the play she was in that she always wears in class, but his are softer, lush, luscious. Everything about him seems like a taste. Is this why Lacey's *Me* magazine cover has "Ten Men to Drool Over"? Could a dumb zine have a clue? Does that writer know anyone like Luis who fills the senses? Black hair, rich as mine is red. Long and scraggly, but cut so it's never in his eyes while he turns. Instead it fans out like a dark halo to frame his head, his head held like a lion's, no, a panther's, on a long, powerful neck. The ridges of his straight nose and high cheekbones catch the light when he demonstrates, the slightest *épaulement* looking so naturally royal. Regal. Only, his lips, thin and straight, with always a slight mocking smile, seem to say, "Me? A prince? A god, you say? No. Nuh-uh, I'm a *man.*"

That's what makes Luis perfect. He's human. He's real. He's powerful. And I swear, when he touched my hip, just one finger to remind me to turn out the standing leg on *ronds de jambe*, I felt powerful. So powerful I thought I would die and dance to heaven. That is so incredibly dumb. I mean: at that moment I felt what it is to be fully alive. One touch does that. Again and again.

He says he'll do a partnering class with me and Thaddeus, Henry, and Naheema. And then, just before pointe class, before Clara arrives, he stands behind me, *sou-sou* right foot front, he says. His hands at my waist, I do what he says, *développé* front, complete *rond de jambe, arabesque effacée, penchée.* I feel weightless. He raises my body and supports me against his chest. Then I do a *pas de bourée* into fourth and I feel his gentle confident support as I do a simple outside pirouette with his hands at my waist. This then is dancing! I want more of this.

Thaddeus, who's been sitting with Lacey in Ursula's office drooling over Desmond Richardson's photo on the cover of *Dance*, calls out, "Bravo."

Later, after pointe class, Lacey sings Clara's praises. "At least she demonstrates instead of doing this"—she indicates steps using her hands like quick little flippers (it's true, Luis does this, but we all know what he means)—"and then leaping full out to show off."

Poor Lacey. Unlike her, I am not intimidated by excellence.

9

AT SUPPER DAD MENTIONS THE POSSIBILITY OF BUYING some acres of hayfield from Clay's mother. Grampa says, "Woe to those who add house to house and join field until everywhere belongs to them and they are the sole inhabitants of the land. Isaiah 5:8."

I gather that's his vote.

Mom goes, "God knows we have enough to do already." I guess we're on a religious theme.

Dad says he thinks they need the money but maybe he'll offer to rent the fields, not buy them; Clay might want them someday.

It's Ash Wednesday. Grammy used to take me for ashes. No one mentions it this year. Dust to dust. Cleaning out the stove this morning I put on my own ashes. The only one who noticed was Clay, at chores. *Dust thou art and to dust thou shalt return*, he said, pulling me close and holding my face in his two hands. He gazed at the smudge on my forehead and then into my eyes. My face felt enflamed. He kissed me. His lips hot against my forehead, my eyes, my cheeks, my mouth. *Not dust but clay*, he said, smoothing his hands like a sculptor down my back, around my body. Solid and strong, of earth, of life. My priest of earth, of life, not death. That's what Rodin would do.

What Clay really said was, "Your face is dirty," and motioned to his own forehead.

What I really said was, "How come your name is Clay?" but he didn't hear me over the milk pump. It's not him I want anyway. I don't know why I think of him at all.

I retreat to the haymow and *grand jeté* across the floor. It's February 29. Leap Year—I love the name. By this late in winter I can dance around in the hayloft. Not my cramped attic "studio" above the milk house, but in the beautiful lofty haymow itself. On the open floor where the bales are fed out, I've swept a place and it's sweet. It's a great, sacred space with a floor of wooden boards tucked together, no cement under it, just air and cows. It's very slippery from dust and chaff, but I bring a damp towel and wet my shoes. It works slick, but not too slick. The roof arches over me, opening all this space. A late-February barn more than half empty of feed and not needed till June for the new crop. More precious than a church; God hangs out here. I bring my CD player and go up early afternoon or late after dinner when there's no one but me and cows in the barn.

Luis says I need to practice constantly. Today I work on pirouettes and spotting. I leap. I do all the combinations I can remember. Pigeons flap out of the way and then coo in the rafters. Sparrows flutter applause on the wing. Ghosts sit impressed on the remaining hill of hay bales at the far end. Dust shows in the light beams around me. But here I am more than dust.

Dad happens to come up and whistles softly. Smiling, he tells me we've got the cleanest haymow around. Grampa G.W., behind him, says, "Take care, the floor's slippery as grease," but also tells me today I look like an angel of God flitting around. That's in spite of the J.W. thing. I doubt they're big into angels. I could be wrong.

Mom shouts from below, "Kitty, throw down twenty bales, if it's not too much trouble." What a tone! I can't keep dancing after a comment like that. Air out of the proverbial balloon. The birds vanish; the dust settles. My legs disintegrate. I become dust.

"We got it," Dad says to me, but the spell is broken.

Being dust I walk solemnly to that other, more private space for a studio, the attic above the milk house, and consider. It's heaped with stuff—old burlap feed bags, harness crap from Grampa's horses, odd pipes and pieces of stanchions. Everything seems heavy, incredibly cobwebby, layered with dust. Where does it all come from? I hate to think. They say house dust is mostly dead skin. Here, maybe dead flies, spiders, cowhide, bird feathers, and poop—all on its way to becoming nothing.

It would take two or three people a whole week to throw the stuff out the swinging door/window onto the driveway and another day to haul the metal to the scrap place and sort through the rest. No one here has time. I don't have enough arms. I'm too weak. Tonight I can't do a double pirouette, my most depressing moment this week.

I got the sense that for Ursula dance is a prayer. This was the gospel according to Ursula as I remember it and hear it in my head: *Your body is a temple. It is your instrument and must be tuned sharp, pure, clear. No alcohol, no drugs, no smoking. I know you don't want to hear that, many disagree, but it's true. There must be discipline in your life, and dance is the place to put it to practice. Then it will become second nature. Practice discipline. It will give you freedom. Freedom. Freedom, you all want it. But freedom is not license, my teacher Hanya Holm always said. Freedom is the earned ability to do what you most desire to do. Earned with the practice of discipline. Am I wind in the woods? Hot air to you? Do you have the faintest idea what I am talking about? Hello?*

Class with Luis focuses on *what* we do and *how,* not why. For Luis it's about peak performance. Art, I guess. Today he goes to Michelle, "Show us the inside of your ankle. The inside of your thigh. Ah, you have tiny turnout. Minuscule! But ah, the malleolus! The loveliest bone in the body, the fetlock of a horse. What in a cow, eh, Kit?"

I can't think. It's not so lovely in a cow. I mumble, "Dewclaw, maybe?"

"Ah, 'Dewclaw, maybe,' says the farm girl, hmm. Well, it's lovely and strong and vulnerable at the same time. Like your neck. Very powerful, very sexy. Show it to us, *present* it to us. Ooh, I want to take all those ankles and kiss them." He drops Michelle's, takes mine. And kisses it. I can't breathe.

I remember everything Ursula said, but I *feel* everything Luis says.

10

When I ask Mom again about the audition, she simply says, "No." She won't talk about it at all. Just "No."

I walk up high into the sugar woods, and scream to drown out those crazy nuthatches hammering around upside down knocking their heads out, for what? Bugs. I scream till my throat hurts and I bet Dad down in the barn can hear me and is telling Grampa G.W., *Oh that's Kit screaming in the woods.* And Grampa tells Dad, *Yup, scream, scream, let out the steam,* even though he can't hear squat.

They think they know me. If they knew how I felt they'd be screaming too. Dad, all the way to divorce court. Grampa, in an infanticidal rage, would choke his only child, my mother. My mother my mother my mother my mother. The worm. The snake. Evil evil insidious passive-aggressive Cyn. I see another life like a light ahead and she turns it off. *Click.*

At dinner with more witnesses I take a breath, calm my heart, and say, "I know you don't like the idea right off the bat, Mom, but, Dad, Luis thinks I'm good enough so I should be dancing more, like every day, at that special school. And like I told you, the audition is soon, March fifteenth."

"Kit, I already said no," Mom says.

"Yeah, but Dad should get a say; Grampa too." I try to lighten the tone and wink at Grampa.

Mom ignites. "No means no, Kit. You're too young to go away to some fancy school just because some substitute dance teacher thinks it might be nice. What does he know about what we want?"

"What you want? What about what *I* want?" I scream this, unfortunately. I lose Dad's sympathy.

"Kitty, calm down and just explain," he says. "I don't get it."

But I have to leave the table with her horrible food and her horrible face. I run to my room, slam the door, and fall to the floor, writhing. All gut, all pain. *Movement never lies.* Did Martha Graham mean pain like this? Whisper sniffs at my face and licks tears. I stuff him out the door. I need more than that. Maybe I should write a poem and roll it up and stuff it in a plastic milk jug and float it in the precious bulk tank. My letter saying, *Bye bye, screw you. I've been a good sport till now but I'm done.* Then I'll do what she says I can't do. I'm going anyway. I'm going to the audition and I'm going to get in.

I want to talk to someone, but not Lacey. This is what she would expect of my family. I want Luis to appear, or even the Clay-like person of my imagination that I'm actually close to. Or even little Timmy. But I can't conjure them now. There is nobody. I prostrate myself on my bed.

What I think ineffably unfair is that there are couples all over the world—men and women mostly, I guess, but also men with men and women with women—sleeping side by side. It's so damn … tender. Even if they are sad or were fighting, or are sick or have problems at work, while asleep they have company. All I've got are stuffed animals like my ratty old Pegasus here, but just think of a warm, breathing human being for comfort!

Grownups—even the ugly ones like Mom and Laura Pizer at the video store, who just got married (there seems to be someone for almost everyone!)—don't know how lucky they are. They don't act delighted enough. If I were them I'd just always be so comforted, so cozy.

I promise if I ever have kids they will have a parent who acts as happy as she should. And remembers what it is like to be fifteen. I promise to remember. I vow.

I get up and open the door to Whisper, who's been scratching.

Next day I hear a big fight, the only yelling one I can remember:

Come on, Cyn, this costs us. I'll do it.

Are you saying I can't do anything right?

Jesus, Cyndy!

Don't say Jesus unless you mean to pray.

God, okay, just stop moping and pay on time. What's the problem?

You don't know anything about it.

Jesus!

It's after lunch and they're in the kitchen; I'm in the living room recliner reading Isadora Duncan's *My Life* with the TV picture on, sound off. Whisper is bunched on the sofa Buddha-like, eyes open, unmoving. I am still feeling raw from last night; now I feel worse. Then, amazingly, Dad leaves, actually goes to their room, thumps around up there, comes down with a duffel bag, goes to the bathroom, clanks around, storms out the kitchen door, and speeds off in the truck.

The house dies down like a doused fire. "Where'd Dad go? Why's he mad?" I call to Mom in the kitchen.

She comes to the living room and shrugs. "I paid some bills late, got finance charges." She lies down, curls up hugging Whisper.

I can't figure out how Mom can sleep. I wait, watch Oprah's face exude emotion. I stretch a little. No dance today, but I'm almost relieved. I still feel shocked. It gets to be three or four. Mom wakes, shakes her head when I start to ask about Dad, glides into the kitchen. She makes tea. She eats cookies, drinks tea, keeps checking at the window. It gets to be four-thirty. "We better start chores," she says. "No Clay today, and Grampa's gone to get sawdust." I'd like to say, You drive *everyone* away, but I can't quite spit the words out. Did I drive Dad away?

We go to the barn and get to work. She feeds corn; I scrape and bed the cows, and then we milk, stepping across full gutters.

After about six cows are done, Dad arrives. He looks at me, then at Mom. She lifts her hand in his direction and turns back to Mercy, the cow she's under. He smiles. He goes to run out the manure.

I feel only relief.

11

ISADORA SAYS SHE LOVED THE SEA, AND THAT MOUNTAINS gave her "a vague feeling of discomfort and a desire to fly … a desire to leap over them and escape." Her mother, she wrote, "was too busy to think of any dangers which might befall her children … and to this wild, untrammelled life of my childhood … I owe the inspiration of the dance I created, which was but the expression of freedom." How can my mother be so busy and still think of dangers?

Isadora was also into astrology, so today I read this horoscope for me: *VIRGO (Aug. 23–Sept. 22). You may feel alone on your path but you're not. You've got key people on your side. What you know, you know well. You'll find love while learning about what you don't know.*

Key people—I feel the truth of these words in my gut. It's fate that Luis has come into my life. I sit next to him today while we watch a film of Martha Graham's *Letter to the World* based on Emily D.'s poems. That's what I needed to do the other night: write a letter to the world. Better yet, dance one.

Crackling with energy, the old B&W film is part of Naheema's senior project. It starts with two women in white, perfectly draped dresses, a dancer and a speaker. *I'm nobody! Who are you? Are you nobody, too? Then there's a pair of us,* says the speaker. A piano plays. The movement is odd and formal but full of weightless jumps with perfect *ballon.* You can hear the squeak of the wood floor. *I'm sorry for the dead today.* A tall woman in black holds the dancer/child in white who dies. Hymn tunes and a stiff funeral. The child awakes and does a shrugging dance, maybe to get rid of death. Then comes a guy after her; the tall mother figure chops space between them, eliminates him. The girl dances pain and the speaker says, *Of course I prayed and did God care ...* The dancer puts her hand to her cheek—*After great pain a formal feeling comes*—and does a *pas de deux* with mother/death, who leaves her alone on stage, sitting, hands together. *This is my letter to the world, that never wrote to me.* I wonder if Emily Dickinson was whiny, or just lonely, or a showoff? It's not ballet, but as I watch I feel the power in my gut. I also feel company. Luis's arm brushes against mine, ever so lightly.

After the movie Naheema lends me Martha G.'s auto-biography, *Blood Memory*. "To balance the ballet," she says, with a glance at Luis. Some of the pictures in the book are very cool. There's one of Helen Keller with Martha G., ringed by dancers as though they're playing a game, and she's the radiant cheese standing alone in the center of a dance she can't see but—obvious from the look on her face—can feel. Dance is a feeling. Maybe that's why I'd rather dance than watch dance. I didn't go to the Momix performance at the college last week. But I didn't have a ride either.

Luis says in class, "Competition is good. Say 'I'm better than you' to the other girls. Yes, you must be all that you can be."

He is talking to me, I know. The audition is three weeks away. I still don't have permission, but I tell him I keep forgetting to bring in the application. He doesn't know I scream in the woods in frustration. We don't talk much. But when he looks at me, he listens with his eyes. I can tell he wants to know all about my soul. Okay, Lacey says he's got the hots for me. I tell Lacey, "He's married! To just the most gorgeous dancer we've ever seen."

I'm not stupid. I don't encourage him. I didn't kiss *his* hand. I know what's up. He's probably just playing around in his dramatic way, a different way from, say, Dad, or Clay and his band of buds. They are so … pedestrian. Rules of morality are made for them. One man, one woman. Otherwise no one would stick with Mom and cows. Farm life needs commitment. I'm kind of surprised Jesus wasn't a dairy farmer. His rules suit the life. What did those people do besides fish and watch sheep by night?

Anyway, that's different from the life of the imagination, where you follow feeling and truth and through it create lasting art. Luis is an artist. Can I help loving how his attention makes me feel? Like an artist too, deep into the earth and taller than the clouds. What I feel makes me expand beyond the limits of ordinary life. It feels holy.

I haven't done a thing wrong. I exist, inspire, and feel. And, oh yeah, work my butt off in class.

Lacey just doesn't like him. I have finally discovered she is dating Mike. Mike! Clay's friend, pothead, snow-pissing Mike. So there you have it.

PART THREE

1

IT SHOULD HAVE BEEN SIMPLE. LUIS MADE ALL THE
arrangements. He spoke to the people at the Academy
about me, and when he put the application into my hands
as if it were the map to a treasure, he looked directly into
my eyes and said, "Kityana, this would be good for you."
He got this kid named Clive from Film Studies to tape me
in a class and edit it so I looked really good; he signed me
up for the audition March 15, the Ides of March. *Beware the
Ides of March.* I remember that from Latin class, but I don't
remember the specifics. My part, he said, was to fill out the
application, get my parents to sign and send a deposit, get
my body ready, and live with the jitters.

After class today he stops me and gives another eye-to-
heart treatment. "Kit," he says, "I called L'Académie to see
if they got Clive's tape, and they said they never got your
application. The audition is less than two weeks away. You
don't seem like the sort to forget. We've taken care of everything else. Help us out here. What's the problem?"

He's looking down at me, not unkindly, but I feel
opaque. Why can't I describe my roadblock at home, and
her mate? It seems so juvenile; I should be able to handle
them.

"No problem," I say. "I'll send it today."

On the way home, desperate, I say to Mom, "I'm asking
nicely, please. I can't accept no as an answer."

"Kit, look. You dance plenty here. It's enough. No means no."

"This would be different," I tell her. "I'd learn so much more. Classes are all day, not just ballet but modern and jazz and music and all the important subjects too like math and science and English. And French, of course."

"Oh, French. Of course," she says.

I switch to Dad, old buddy, parent of last resort. We do chores side by side alone. Grampa's tapping his line of maples, Clay has a playoff basketball game, Mom's cooking or helping Grampa. I wait till after milking when Dad sits for a minute on a bale listening to the end of Clay's game on WDEV and watching Big Poppy, his favorite cat, lap milk. I sit close beside him and hand him the application and a pen.

"Sign here, please." I'm counting on distraction, but he takes the paper and reads it with squinty attentiveness as if it were a flyer on robotic milkers.

"What's this?" He shifts under the dim bulb a bit. Grampa insists we stick to sixty watts. "Well, hell, Kitty, we don't have fifteen thousand dollars. Even Canadian." He hands the paper back. "I think you and your mother been round this track."

I try telling him that Luis said a school like that in the States would be $25,000 or more, but he stares at Veritec and Manny jostling each other to get at the milk and I can see the bargain angle is no selling point. "Luis said there's a good chance I could get a scholarship. He knows the director and had a video of me made and I've filled out the application and Luis said he would bring me to the audition and all you have to do is sign. I'll pay the application fee. Please, just sign."

He starts scratching his head all over, chasing the hay chaff out, I guess, and resettles his hat, sighing deeply. Clay's team is losing by fifteen points, which is unfortunate for the mood. "Well, if you can pay your way and it's really what you want, Kit, I guess we ought to let you give it a try. I would sure miss you."

"Me too," I say, "thank you," and hug him. He signs, and when we get to the house, writes a check for $50, and won't take the five tens I try to hand him.

Uh-oh. Those acts created a rift, you might say, between him and Mom. I gather they had discussed it before and *agreed on no.* All night she pouts and scowls and says, "I can't believe it," a million times. Faith destroyed. In me, nothing new. But in him? She's nasty, vituperative, bitchy. I hear *Over her dead body,* and *Why,* and *Who will do her chores,* and *What kind of people send a fifteen-year-old away? People who don't want them, that's who,* and the crowning blow of rhetoric hitting Dad down and dirty: *Why is this Luis character doing all this anyway, have you thought about that, Don Snow?*

Ooh, she's good, *mama mia,* she's crafty and almost convincing perhaps, had I not exploded from the living/eavesdropping room. "He's a teacher, Mom, and a really good dancer. I know it's hard for you to believe this, but he thinks *I'm* a really good dancer and this school would be the best place for me to get better. He and his wife taught there, as I have told you but you weren't listening. Why are you so anti-school? They're leaving Hope Springs in June, who knows if Ursula will be able to teach. He's trying to help. It's his *job* to help. If you're so worried, talk to him or Ursula. You like her, don't you? You worry about everything. You *like* to worry."

"That's *my* job," she spits back at me. Then she, quick as a hawk, grabs the sealed, stamped envelope from my hand, and in one strike tears the form with Dad's signature and the check in half. Unbelievable.

I pull the pieces from her claws and run outside. An ill-timed snow squall traps me quick, but I retreat to Grampa's trailer. He says, "Come in, come in. Checkers or gin?"

We converse some about sugaring. I try to control my shaky voice. I shuffle the cards but don't deal. I hate to overburden him with gripes about Mom, who is after all his only child. I'm sensitive to that. But I tell him what just happened. I say, "Grampa, I just don't get why she's got to be mean."

"Remember, she's had a hard time of it."

That old song. I *don't* remember. "So have you," I say.

"Me? I'm on easy street; your folks do most of the work, Walyo keeps me good company, and I got an angel watching over all." He's looking at an unframed 4 x 6 of Grammy that's propped against a mug on the TV. She's looking up from weeding, smiling, her gray curls flying around her head. He must have just put it there.

Sometimes I can't stand how sweet he is. But it makes me miss her more. If she were here she'd help me. She always loved to see me dance.

"And you have a friend, right? Roberta." I don't want him to be sad.

He barely skips a beat and says, "Roberta's fine. She's got me reading the Bible more, and that's good. Oh, oh now, now, Rusty." He's patting my head because I'm leaking tears, I'm so frustrated.

Well, he turns out to be the certified miracle worker. He goes to Mom on my behalf, quoting Ecclesiastes 3, verse 4: *A time to cry; a time to laugh; a time to grieve; a time to dance.* Must be the Bible's all-around full report on dance, but if so, it seems to have done the trick.

Then Mom calls Ursula—disturbing her rest, I'm sure. Mom then promptly calls Luis, and I don't know what all he said, but he should have been the one to negotiate the whole thing in the first place because, after telling Dad he should have waited for her to sign, Mom drives to Hope Springs to get a new application. This is all done without her saying to me, *I've changed my mind.* When I tell her thank you, she says thank Grampa and your father, and Ursula. *Against my better judgment*, she mutters. *Let's pray it works out.*

But she and Dad are friendly again. Disgustingly so. They stretch out together on the sofa in the living room late Sunday morning after chores and church and breakfast. Grampa sits nearby like a kid reading the comics and nibbling bacon while Waldo crouches nearby watching each bite and saying please with his tail. Dad's sort of twiddling Mom's stupid white hair. Her eyes are closed. Even Whisper never looks so blatantly needy.

What a cute little family scene! I go on into the kitchen and rattle the lid of the dog-food bin so at least Waldo will come to his senses and follow me.

2

WEEKS BECOME DAYS TILL THE AUDITION. I WORK HARD
in class, on details. Usually I think about the big picture,
what are the steps, what is the feel, or I don't think at all.
But now I study the finer points, the shape carved by Luis's
fingers, the *épaulement* of his head, exactly how high a leg
on *grand battement*, landing in perfect fifth after *assemblé*.
During the few classes Clara teaches I look at her, then at
myself in the mirror, copying everything. I wish that Clara
taught more because she really is the only ballerina I've ever
seen so closely. I realize for the first time how old Ursula
is, and how modern in her approach. That's fine, but for
L'Académie I need Clara's look, her lines.

I'm really careful about eating. No chocolate. I don't
want zits for the day, and March 15 is right before my period
is due, which is usually not a good time skinwise. Luis tells
me to wear my long-sleeved dark green leotard with the
deep V neck and low back. He gets Clara to show me exactly
how to braid and coil and pin my hair so the bun won't get
wispy. He says we in Vermont have disorderly hair, always.

I figure Clara and Lola are coming too by the way she
says after class, "Don't worry, Marcel is very nice; he likes
us. And we know the perfect café for lunch after."

Only one other person tells me not to worry. As I'm
getting into my coat Thaddeus pushes *Dance* in my face,
open to an article on Wendy Whelan. "She's a Taurus, like

me, very earthy and grounded." His finger points out her words: *I think fate takes you where you want to go and you have to just trust your gut.* He takes his finger from the page and pokes me in the belly. "Fear not, Kitana."

The evening before "A"-Day I was hoping to get chores done early so I could wash my hair in time for it to dry before an early bedtime. I hate sleeping with a wet head.

Dad's cleaning the gutters and bedding cows, Clay's feeding grain, Mom and I are milking. Grampa G.W. is with Roberta boiling sap in the sugarhouse or somewhere, but he did the calves and fed corn and set up the milking equipment before he left. It probably took him all afternoon, he's that slow, and if I'd been in the barn with him I would have gone crazy wishing he'd hurry, and he would have said, *Dilly-dally brings night as fast as hurry-scurry.* But the way it worked out, he was a huge help, kind of like the family elf in the fairy tale who made shoes while the family was sleeping. Grampa watches out for us like a guardian angel. I hope Roberta doesn't take him away from us.

If Mom misses his presence, she doesn't let on. In fact, she just milks along to the music—something in the classic-rock line, Bruce Springsteen maybe. She doesn't even grace me with her usual naggeldy, anxiety-born questions. (*So what time are you leaving? Who's driving? What time will you be home?*) Either she's forgotten about the audition *or* she figures if she ignores the whole thing it will dissolve, *poof,* and this will be our life forever: her, me, Dad, G.W., Clay, the cows, all together forever and ever, amen.

I try to rush, maybe skip dipping a teat or two. Maybe don't hand-strip every last clump from old Mastitis Maggie, as I call her, old Margaret, a favorite of Mom's. Maybe I keep checking the clock, or say shit when Sweetpea swats me with a gutter-dipped tail. I'm half expecting Mom to remind me to use all the steps of our milking protocol, including wearing those damn nitrile gloves because our somatic cell count is up a bit.

"You go," Mom says instead. "I'll finish here."

I am grateful. I say, "I just have a lot to do for tomorrow."

"Do what you like, like what you do." A Grampa quote, it sounds bitter from her mouth.

She doesn't even ask what all I have to do.

A half hour later I've showered, scrubbed, shaved pits and legs, and I smell of hibiscus shampoo. The hand-crank phone from the barn rings, but I ignore it. I'm naked, with only my hair wrapped in a towel, smoothing SkinTrip onto my legs and callused toes, when I hear my name tearing the peace.

"Kit! Kitty!" and then *bang bang bang* on the door. "You in there?"

"What?" My voice sounds flimsy in this place.

"Why didn't you answer the phone? I need you to finish up. Clay needs stitches. I have to take him to the emergency room."

"What? Can't Dad … ?" I start.

"Did you *hear* me? Clay's cut his foot on the gutter cleaner. Badly. Open the door. Now! *Now!*" She sounds hysterical.

I pull on another towel. She pushes past me to grab two more from the rack. Her boots are printing snowy shit and sawdust tracks on the damp floor, a new vinyl floor she laid down last summer, a swirly pattern she said was called Ballet. In her usual and customary mind she'd tar and feather anyone who sullied her floors.

"What happened?"

"Hurreee," she squeals, and exits like a nutcase.

I have no choice. I pull dirty overalls and a jacket over my clean body as quickly as I can and get to the barn just as she and Clay are pulling away in the car, spewing snow and gravel. He gives me a two-finger wave and smiles a half smile. He doesn't look dead, not remotely. More embarrassed.

Dad stands by the milk-house door, looking patient. He's got the look down, thumbs tucked in his back pockets, gazing down at a rubbing cat (Schilling, maybe), nudging it with his boot. The cat scoots when it sees me. It knows I'm not a Sox fan in any significant way. Dad tells the tale, as calm as Mom was panicky.

"He slipped on the reverse corner while he was carrying milk to the calves. Sliced his ankle on a gutter paddle. Milk spilled. Had on some damn falling-apart shoes. Prob'ly does need a stitch or two, tetanus shot. Mostly, she's mad."

"At me," I say.

"At life," he says. "Hey, I got this. She didn't need to call you. She didn't need to go herself. Clay could drive with one damn leg."

I help finish anyway, 'cause he didn't ask and there wasn't much left to do.

But Mom isn't done. She taps on my half-closed door as I'm brushing my hair before bed, and before I can ask how's Clay, she says, "Just one thing, Kit. I'm going to drive you tomorrow. Dad and I decided it would be best."

I have to hand it to her: I did not see that one coming. She has floored me. I stop breathing.

She plows ahead, oblivious to my heart attack, lifts her pointy chin, and rattles on, "I'll call Luis right now to get directions. What's his last name again? I don't have his number."

"No," I say, when I can. Every cell in my body is saying no. "This is the most ridiculous thing you have ever done. He's the teacher. He made all the arrangements. He *has* to be there. You'll be causing him and Clara huge inconvenience."

"Oh, I don't think so, Kit. Who wouldn't want to be saved six hours of driving?" She thinks she's the queen of common sense, sounds so sure of herself.

I shrug. "Then I might as well not go. He has to be there. Teachers have to accompany their students. Maybe you didn't see that on the application, on the information sheet."

"What information sheet?" She's suspicious, but I've slowed her down.

"Never mind." I push past her. "I'll call Luis and tell him it's all off. Is that what you want?"

"Kitty, stop." She grabs my arm and I yank it away. "Just tell him I'm coming along with you."

Another blast with the stun gun, this one subtle. I pause. What she suggests is not crazy, but I have lived with a picture of tomorrow and she is not in it. I will not surrender.

"Yah, sure—you, me, Luis, Clara, and Lola, in his Honda Civic for six hours. That should be comfortable. I'll be in great shape to dance. Or would you like to take our truck, put Lola on the roof? Just forget it. Just let me call them so they can change their plans and stop trying to help me. Ever again." I head down the stairs.

"Kit. Stop." She looks white and hard as marble, very still. "I didn't realize the teacher had to be there. And his family is going. Now I understand. Okay? Leave it. Sleep well."

I look at her standing two steps above me, dandelion fluff, absurd like a Silkie, and I'm almost sorry too. "Okay," I say. And then, "Thanks. You too."

3

By the time my alarm rings I am more than ready to go and never return. I am also tired. I didn't sleep well, in spite of using all the relaxation exercises I know and the incantation *Rest, you need to rest.* At five-thirty the March light is barely awake, soft and fuzzy, the way I look in the bathroom mirror as I brush my teeth and put in my contacts.

Mom and Dad have finished their coffee and he's heading to the door. "Big day," he says and squeezes me in a one-armed hug. "Give 'em hell. Break a leg. Isn't that what you're supposed to say?"

I see Mom grimace at that. She stays silent and distant but offers her precious eggs scrambled or fried. Even though it's too early for my ride I politely decline breakfast and head down the driveway to wait. From the doorway she calls after me, "Good luck," and then adds, "Kit, I mean it."

I wave back to her and I mean to smile, but I don't know if it shows. The icy snow crunches under foot a few inches deep, but the cold doesn't seem real. Redwing blackbirds, even robins, chitter already. The air smells of wood smoke and sap vapor from the tiny sugar shack behind Grampa's trailer. Shivering by the mailbox, I wait alone for my ride, my prince and the royal family.

When the Honda pulls up, Luis is alone, no Clara, no baby. I hop inside quickly, although there's no chance Mom could see into the car from the house. I start, "Where—?"

"Ah," he says, "too far for Lola." It's warm in the car, then thrillingly so as heat from the car seat touches my butt. I almost say something, but Luis smiles and raises his black brows. "Ready? You look ready. I should have guessed, the farm girl is a morning person."

He stops first at Maplefields for coffee and gas. "Want some?" he asks. I tell him I don't drink either, but he doesn't hear my joke. He comes back with two cups. "Black for me. Green for you." At first I think only of gas puddling iridescently, but the cup is warm and fragrant. "Tea," Luis says. "Very good for you."

By the time we bump over the familiar Greensbrook and Hope Springs roads and head north on the interstate, I'm feeling queasy and my contacts are already scratching my tired eyes. All night Whisper was curled right where my legs should go, so I was angled to the side or straddling him. Then I got up at four-thirty to take a bath and braid and coil my hair the way Clara showed me. I repacked my bag with the green leotard, tights, extras, soft slippers, pointe shoes, scissors, tape, lambswool, brush, CD player, headphones, CDs, a Balance bar, two apples, a water bottle, tweezers, tampons, a notebook, the papers the school sent with the audition confirmation and advice that "getting a good night's sleep is the best way to prepare," and $150, my saved money. I had a feeling I would need all my resources for this day.

Luis says it's a nice morning. It is, I agree. But that sounds lame. I tell Luis how once last year I ran away. On a March morning like this, only earlier, before my parents woke up, I walked and hitched into Greensbrook and spent a week staying at different friends' houses. It was very cool to see how other people live, I tell Luis.

"What did your parents do?" Luis asks.

I tell him I left them a note saying not to worry. They called around a little, of course, but my dad finally convinced my mother to relax and wait. "Leave 'em alone and they'll come home," my grandfather apparently advised. And when I did, they seemed to treat me less like a little kid.

"You amaze me," Luis says, toasting me with his coffee cup.

I'm glad I made up that little story for our entertainment. I truly *did* consider such a sojourn into civilized life after Grammy died, but I didn't know a house to go to where a parent wouldn't call my mother, notorious mama hen. I know some parents cover for other kids all the time. Why not for me? They're afraid of Mom, I think, or afraid for her. It stinks, everyone knowing our business.

Luis, being new, doesn't know all this. He drives on, humming, past a "Champlain Islands" sign, past a weigh station.

I think of Mom in the kitchen sticking a brown bag into my backpack even though I packed what food I wanted. Then she's at the door waving, a small, pinched animal peeping in a foreign language, "Good luck. Kit, I mean it." I felt sorry for her. Those words couldn't touch me.

I must have dozed till just before the border. Luis tugs

gently on my arm. "Hey, Kityana, wake up now. Canada may want to talk to you. Get out your ID."

Shit. I tell him I forgot.

"What?" he says. "I told you passport, birth certificate, license, something."

Well, it doesn't matter because after "*Bonjour*" Luis launches into a flood of French greetings or jokes or other pleasantries, judging by the nodding and smiling of the border guard. A woman, *bien sûr*. I knew he spoke ballet French but had no idea he was fluent. He babbles along till I hear "Hope Springs College" and "*danseur*" and then motions to me and says something about L'Académie des Arts.

"*Eh, pour le ballet?*" she says, looking at me. I try to simultaneously sit up straighter and lean forward so I can smile to her sweetly and I hope reassuringly. My bun still looks balletic, I guess, and she nods. "Carrying any mace or pepper spray?" she incongruously asks, and when I say no, calls, "*Et bien, bonne chance,*" as she waves us onward.

"They are worse coming into the States," Luis says, no longer smiling. "After 9/11."

By now it's almost eight o'clock, gray daylight and cold. I recognize, a little, the lay of the land from the trip Dad and I took to check out the robot. Same flat fields, corn stubble poking through snow patches, same *ferme* houses with bright yellow or blue doors kissing the roadside. Compared to Vermont, fewer trees and more electric lines and billboards edge the flat, narrow road.

We drive in more traffic now, but Luis keeps pace with

the natives, past corn cribs and *maize sucre* signs, barns that look like factories, a stone church with a gray roof matching the silver of the sky, a huge statue of a guy wearing a Coke T-shirt.

Something must be wrong with the car's heater. My palms are sweating, but my teeth are chattering and my head begins to ache.

Maybe Luis thinks I'm nervous because he starts to sing: *I'll build a stairway to paradise, with a new step ev'ry day*, and "I Got Rhythm" and "Shall We Dance" and a bunch of other old songs that make me laugh. Stuff from Mom's musicals. I can't believe he knows them.

Then suddenly he pulls over to the narrow shoulder of the *autoroute*, puts the car in Park, looks at me and says, "Turn that way," and motions toward my window.

I turn, ever *l'étudiante*, and see nothing but a scraggly oasis of poplar trees around a stone house. I feel his warm hands. They start kneading the knots in my neck, and then massage and smooth from there. Both shoulders through my poofy too-hot down jacket, my upper arms, back to my painful, tender neck, bare under his touch. And then my temples and eye sockets. I wince. "My contacts."

"Oh, yes," he says. All the worried and aching places he seems to know about. He ends with a kiss at the nape of my neck that I feel down through my gut to the length of my stubby toes. I'm thinking, *The day is good; the day will be perfect.*

Except the kiss doesn't happen. His massage has

dislodged a contact, and I have to reposition it using the little mirror on the visor.

He doesn't seem to notice. "That will be better," he says. He resumes driving and after a while starts talking about him and Clara meeting in New York and working at L'Académie. At some point he scoops my hand into his and pulls it to rest on his muscular thigh. I sit a little lopsided, off center, and my head, though better, still hurts.

I can't focus on what else he talks about as we enter the city. My stomach growls and I want to use my hand to get food from Mom's brown bag, which is closer than my backpack, but I'm feeling carsick, so I don't. Luis yawns and says he's ready for breakfast and *café au lait* and maybe a nap. I reclaim my hand, open the bag, and offer him potluck. "From my mother," I say, just then noticing the folded paper tucked into the bag: a copy of my birth certificate, gift of *ma mère*.

"Good," Luis says when I show him.

There are also three muffins and three hardboiled eggs and two baggies, one with dry cereal and one with apple slices sprinkled with cinnamon. The second one is sort of a brown sticky mess, but the smell when I open the bag seems to repair my stomach.

Luis eats two muffins (raspberry) in a flurry of crumbs and ecstatic murmurings: "Oh, oh, oh, I must marry your mother. And you grew these berries … Oh, oh, mmmfgh."

It feels so good to laugh at him. I ask how long since his last meal. At that moment, as I slowly sniff, then lick, then chew a single apple slice, Luis seems very like a boy my age. "Look at the wires," he says, pointing to the roadside, "like men on stilts parading along the road."

"Like robots," I say.

"A high-voltage launching pad for rockets," he says.

A herd of power towers, I almost say, but he quickly changes tune.

He says, "Now to get ready, you must start to breathe and wake up your body. Drink some water. Sit up taller, uncross those legs, close your eyes, and take a deep, long breath, feeling the air go down your throat, chest, diaphragm, abdomen, pelvis, and all the way through your thighs and knees to your calves, ankles, the arches of the feet, the toes—Kit, yes, are you breathing?—and then out slowly till you are empty. And again, let me hear, this time sending air into the fingertips and again breathing into every space in your lovely head. Again," and he guides me through just what I need to shed the ache and torpor of the early rising, the long drive, the fear of what's to come.

As we cross a huge bridge he starts telling funny stories about Montreal, the students, their landlady who was a drug dealer. By the time we wind through traffic in the city, park the car, and walk through spitting sleet to the gray stone steps of L'Académie, I am wide awake.

4

THIS PLACE IS UNLIKE MY PUNY WOODEN ELEMENTARY school, unlike the Greensbrook High warehouse, unlike the brick and clapboard Hope Springs College. As soon as we push open the door I feel warmth and splendor. A huge chandelier lights a carpeted hallway dominated by a towering grandfather clock and an elegant stairway spiraling away to the upper floors. Piano music floats around like a spirit, welcoming me. The smell of Endust (probably from the clock and the banister and the armchairs sitting sentry in the lobby) reminds me of Hope Springs. Someone does a fine job of cleaning here. Mom would be impressed.

Luis of course knows the ropes and leads me into an office where a lady with very black, very short hair and very long red fingernails takes my name and matches it against a list on her desk. A long list I read upside down, titled "B-Group Audition, 10:00." She then puts a second check at "9:20, Katherine Snow" on a short list headed "Interviews—M. Laliberté."

"I have an interview?" I look to Luis.

"*Naturellement*," he says.

This is not among my expected morning chores.

"I thought I was just dancing." For some reason the idea of having to talk here panics me. I can't imagine saying anything that would make sense in this environment.

"It's an honor, Kityana, calm down, relax. To meet the

teacher before the class is a very big advantage. He is doing this as a favor to me."

"You can go right in, Katherine," Ms. Black Hair says. Katherine? Did I write that on the form? I remember now that Mom filled out most of the second form after her consultations with Ursula and Luis.

"Aren't you coming?" I ask Luis.

"Only parents." Black Hair holds the door for me, looks toward Luis.

He shoos me forward with his arms as he backs away. "After, Martine will send you upstairs to the studio." He smiles at her.

"Martine" watches him—with amusement, I think—run lightly up the elegant stairs. To me she says, "Mr. Laliberté is waiting."

His office is filled with dark wood, glossy photos, a soft chair that makes me feel short and spineless, and Mr. L.'s crooked and yellow teeth. Maybe it's the angle I get from my very uncomfortable perch, but those teeth are totally prominent and distracting, as are the pictures of dozens of dancers on the walls. Most are doing something impossible like standing on pointe in perfect *attitude à la derrière* or leaping in one-hundred-eighty-degree *grand jeté*. The shiny desk itself is empty of everything but a reflection of Mr. L.'s head and a lonesome paper that looks to be a childishly printed application with my parents' illegible signatures.

He asks me—in English, thank God—lots of questions about classes, what I know, what I like, what ballets I've seen, why I want to come to the Academy, what my parents think, and so on. He's disappointed not to meet them today. He says he liked the video, especially how comfortable and confident I appeared. He says I make dancing look easy and fun. I guess I answer, mostly half eager/half dreading flashes of those yellow teeth when next he speaks.

"Well then, see you in class," he says and directs me past Martine's empty desk and upstairs to the locker room. Well, hardly a locker room. Another far cry from either Greensbrook High or Hope Springs College. The former has a locker room; the latter has a closet-sized changing room with a few coat hooks and a foggy mirror. This place has a Dressing Room, complete with wooden cubbies and benches, also sparkling showers and stalls and sinks, plenty of lighted mirrors, and a Degas dancer tying her shoe on the wall. A pack of middle-school-aged girls are giggling and chatting and fixing their hair and smiling at their reflections. We are given numbers on small rectangles of paper to pin to the front of our leotards. Ah, just like when I show a cow, now I'm feeling at home, although at the fair I have a harness for my numbers and don't mess with pins. Then too, at the fair, the animal, not me, is on display.

The studio has the shine of a church, beautiful smooth maple floor and lots of long windows. I lie on the floor to stretch, surrounded by more girls chattering in hushed voices, all in black leotards and makeup and some with flowers in their hair. One, with flowers *and* makeup, whispers to me, "We're supposed to wear black."

"Oh," I say. Thanks, Luis.

And there he is, standing way at the end of the long room behind a couple of rows of parents in folding chairs, also chatting, with Martine. I say parents, but they are mothers, no doubt about it, although they don't look like mine. These women look sharp, stylish, and pretty, and like razors that could slice each other to shreds. One with henna-red hair sits, legs crossed, in a tiny skirt and wool cape, staring at me with a smirk on her face. Or maybe she's staring at the mirror behind me because she suddenly smooths her hair around her ear. The thought of my mother among them actually makes me smile. I can almost hear her sighing and thinking if they'd start on time they could end on time.

The class is not hard, but I'm sucky, probably from nerves. I don't know, maybe I do okay. The teacher is blond and kind of vapid but has a gorgeous, lithe dancer's body. Everything is simple, clear, the ritual I know. A lady with silver curls like Grammy's after a perm perches at the piano. She keeps smiling as she plays. The *pliés* are simple, starting in second, very slow, two *demis*, two *grands*, *cambre* away from the barre and toward the barre, first, fifth with *cambre* forward and back, with rises and balance.

Mr. L. watches from the front of the room near the door, pad of paper in hand. He doesn't stay the whole time but keeps jumping up and wandering out the door. At the beginning he announced, "Of course you are nervous, but in the long run the class is for you, not the teacher, and not for me. Use what is here. We want to see how you work, not how you show off. That can come later." He flashed those lemony incisors. Why, Grandfather, what yellow teeth you have!

Partway through I catch the piano lady's eye. Then she winks at me. Why? I wonder. Does she see I wear no makeup? That my leotard is green and I'm too tall with the biggest boobs in class? And that's only to say how *young* everyone else is, because I am no Victoria's Secret prospect. Does she guess I'm distracted by teeth?

Or maybe she knows I'm falling in love with her music, because I am. Or maybe I'm focusing on the music because she keeps winking at me during *ronds de jambe*, which are luscious, during *développés*, during *frappés*, which I usually love, but I hit the floor too hard on the first one and hurt my foot, get a charley horse. Why is it called that? Grampa would know. Why am I screwing up? Well, she's *frappé*-ing that piano and I want to do what the music says, but I'm not used to the *immediacy* of live music, and I can hear as well as feel my foot thud like a tripping clod. The tiny, doll-like girl behind me must see. The mothers surely do. Luis seems to have left the room, as has Mr. L. Couldn't they just sit down and watch?

At least I know the sequence of the class. Like Sister Beatrice in CCD at St. Jude's always said: "The great thing about Mass is that it's the same all over the world. You will always feel at home in a Catholic church." Ursula once said the same about ballet class. Seems true. I sort of feel at home.

Too much thinking; I know it. Then the lady winks at me again after a lyrical adagio during which I try to breathe in the music to keep my balance and avoid choking on the height of everyone else's extensions. I pretend the other girls are little sisters watching me with awe and admiration. They are so little and fragile and brittle like twigs. I am a tree, a willow, supple and strong.

At least my pirouettes are working. Doubles are no trouble, which is lucky because all my little sibling rivals can do them. I think the music makes the sense of *up, up* so clear. I feel it in my bones. And I waltz through *balancé* and *piqué* turns and ace all the jumps, especially the *tombe pas de bourée–glissade–pas de chat* combo, my all-time favorite, which I mentally dedicate to Whisper.

We do only a bit of pointe work at the barre and center, and by the time we get to the end, to *révérence*, I feel gloriously free. I feel other than the diminutive ballerinas with their eye shadow and garlands and, yes, one even has glitter on her cheekbones. I feel like Grampa's big horse Frost out in the pasture with the heifers, standing slightly apart from the herd, maybe a little lonely, but strong and beautiful all the same. In short, it is a wonderful class, because my body feels sweaty and worked, inspired by the music but not even tired.

We applaud the teacher. I have no idea what her name is; she never said. We applaud Mr. L., who reappeared, fortunately, during the big jumps; we applaud Madame Durand at the piano. (Mr. L. says her name.) She smiles sweetly and widens her eyes to include the whole class. No winks.

Maybe I imagined them. Mr. Laliberté speaks privately to one of the tiny bejeweled princesses, who is good—okay, the best—but is short of breath, with cheeks on fire. For stamina, I'm thinking, take a horse, take a tree, take me.

When I emerge from the changing room Mr. L. is surrounded by a flock of mothers. Not mine. Not mine, says the horse as she clip-clops down the stairs in search of the surrogate. Ah, *la bulle*! *Voilà*, I find him down one flight perched on a desk in a lofty, bright room with bookshelves ceiling to floor. In the desk chair sits a dancer, maybe a teacher, with a thick, dark ponytail and pretty except for a beaked, lopsided nose accentuated by a ruby stud in one nostril. Perhaps the nose broke sometime when a partner dropped her.

"Yes, yes? How did it go?" Luis is all questions. He doesn't apologize for leaving. He seems relaxed, at home. I'm a bit surprised.

"So, this is your little friend," says Crooked Nose.

"Kit, Nina Gallas, librarian and teacher *extraordinaire*."

She inspects me closely the way a teacher does, evaluating, it seems to me, every inch. A judge, center ring. My 4-H training kicks in and I smile.

"So, you want to attend the Academy. Have you had the tour?"

I say no, except for the studio and the dressing room and an office. She laughs, so I guess I'm funny.

"Luis, you should show her around. How long are you

staying? Take company class this afternoon," she says to him. "The students will be inspired and Sylvie would love to have you."

She raises her eyebrows meaningfully at Luis. Whatever. I detect mysterious history here beyond my ken. Am I a little kid? I am beginning to lose patience with my shifting role: first too old in class, now too young. I feel annoyingly out of place. Limboland. Did I do well? Okay? Lousy? Who knows?

Luis says we'll tour after lunch. But right now it's already past noon. So what do we do? Eat in the dining room, meet some other kids and teachers? Go to the café Clara mentioned? No. We walk outside with the "librarian" into blowing snow and freezing cold. I slip on the sidewalk in my thin black ankle boots with slick soles and crash into Luis, who says, "Whoa, careful," and steps to the side. No hug. No help. Hands off.

All of a sudden he's basically ignoring me. "Nina" with the bobbing ponytail and the bauble in her crooked nostril has invited us to eat at her place. In her long red suede coat and high green boots, she's elegant, like a rose (but for the nose). She leads us four blocks to her apartment on the sixth floor of a fancy building with a doorman who tips his hat to us and says "Bonjour." He looks just like Huck Simpson, our milk inspector, pointy chin, foxy eyes, except he's wearing a fur hat, not a feed cap.

Nina's apartment I immediately title "City Apartment of an Artist," all scattered with scarves and rugs and pillows smelling of incense. A sweet white cat with long fur blowing gently curls by the heat register in the kitchen. While Nina warms up black bean soup I look out the window at a road winding up into the whiteness of a park. "Mont-Royal," Luis calls from the kitchen doorway. "The top is invisible." Sleet taps at the glass.

I happen to adore black bean soup (we grow the beans), and as I eat I begin to feel marginally better. Nina pours out wine, but when I say, "No thanks, I have a headache," she laughs, a tinkling "Uh-huh," and slides my full glass in front of Luis, then leaves the table and returns with two aspirin. I say oh no, not that bad; she says take them, and goes to the kitchen.

Suddenly I need to know, so I blurt to Luis, "What did you think of the audition?" I want a reflection of the bliss I felt dancing to that wonderful piano.

"Honestly, Kit," he says as Nina sets a glass of water before me, "I was disappointed. Here, you are unpolished. It's the power of context, not your fault. We'll talk about it later."

Stunned, that's what I am. As if he'd used a gun.

After that, Nina and Luis mostly gossip. I don't know any of the people they're talking about; I can't listen, fading in and out of despair and fury. He brings out photos of Clara and Lola.

Nina oohs and coos over Lola. She keeps touching Luis, his fingers, his wrist. He doesn't seem to mind. I might as well not be there. I can't just sit there, so I get up and hover around the room looking at pictures of dancers, Nina in many of them, agile and intense as a hawk, and I plop down on some huge pillows feeling sore and suddenly dead tired.

Then, no kidding, I get this huge nosebleed. A gush of bright blood. Nina's there in a flash. "Oh, oh, blood. Your nose. Ah, ah, the pillows!" She thrusts paper napkins at me. Luis's face wrinkles as though I'd pooped in my diaper.

I swear I have never had a nosebleed before. Dad gets them sometimes in winter, when the air is dry and cold, he says. He'll come in from the barn and be blowing the hay chaff from his nose and start a red flood that will last ages, delaying dinner while he sits still by the woodstove with his head tilted back and toilet paper stuck up his nostrils. That's the extent of infirmity I've seen in him.

Well, this turns out to be a bad time to take after Dad. For one thing, Luis and Nina do not make good nurses. She has to get back to the school to teach a class, and Luis is by this time pretty well lubricated, as Grampa would say, and has morphed into a jerk.

First, he fusses over me in a bossy way—"What do you need? Go in the bathroom. No, not her towel. Here's paper"—until I am left wadded with scratchy tissue paper and sitting on the lid of the toilet breathing through my mouth. Lovely.

As Nina leaves, calling out to me, "Nice to meet you, hope we see you back here soon," Luis says his goodbye or whatever and comes back to the bathroom looking ragged. His eyes are bloodshot, his hair scruffy. He sighs, leaking air, more going out than in. Sighs are deadly negative things.

"I think it's stopped bleeding," I say.

He produces a weak smile that works wonders on his looks. I try to mirror it.

After seeming to study the glass shower door, he opens it, reaches in, and starts the water. "Okay, *ma petite*, just take a shower, get all clean. What a day."

He pulls a thick green towel from the wall cabinet, plops it on my lap, and then lays his hand on my head. A little contact, that's all I want! I look up, and he laughs a little, at my nose plugs, I guess. Is he being nice or mocking me?

He says again, "What a day," and then touches my chin and leans down to kiss me light as a butterfly on my lips. It feels nice. The wine smell is strong.

Like it's a reflex, I kiss back. Until I have to pull away to breathe. I'm surprised but not surprised. It's not like I never imagined kissing him. But not like this, with bloody tusks up my nose. So gross.

He stands up and puts his hand to his mouth, coughs before going out, and pulls the door closed behind him. What just happened? I don't know. I want to shed my skin, my head. I extract the damn plugs from my nose.

Already steam is warming and fogging the room, so I peel off my clothes and get under the streaming shower. I want to melt away. I wanted to stop thinking of how things have not gone exactly according to plan. It's not awful, but it's not glorious. Ahh. Hot water, so hot, divine, the best thing in the world. The water pressure is stronger than at home; Nina's soap smells of roses. Water cure. Baptism. I inhale till my nose seems clear. My stupid self is clean. I close my eyes for one more minute of pelting hot wash and to make sure my contacts don't get washed away.

I feel a breeze and hear a creak. Luis steps in behind me. "Mmm, nice and hot," he says. "Better now, eh?"

I am not imagining this.

I hear myself say, "Um … I was just getting out," but I don't get out. He has taken the soap from my hand and is lathering my shoulders and back, gently. I don't scream, though it occurs to me as an option. It's a scary moment, but not like a nightmare. It's something I have never dreamed about. I feel embarrassingly unrehearsed.

I cover my chest with crossed arms and cringe forward. From behind he lifts one arm and soaps one breast, pausing, cupping my breast; then he replaces my arm and does the other side. He soaps my butt. I feel him crouching behind me, slicking my legs in long strokes and touching my feet, between my toes, tugging gently on each ankle till I lift each foot in turn and let him soap the soles and massage the arches as if he knows exactly which spots are sore.

I think … nothing. I breathe air and water through my mouth. I wish I could feel happy. I wish it *were* a dream. I worry my lenses will fall out.

He stands up and presses close behind me and puts both hands on my belly, one hand spread wide and low till his fingers touch my hair, the other hand firm on my ribcage.

"So beautiful, little Kitty." He kisses my neck.

I lose track of everything but him poking against the small of my back. His hand is between my legs.

I try to turn around. I have to get out. I am water-logged, bloated.

"Don't move," he whispers into the ear he is licking and kissing. No. His is the wrong face, wrong body. I feel too wet and crushed. I squirm and slide into the shower door, which pops open. The whole room is steamy and wet and smells of roses. "You moved," he says.

I grab a green towel. I say nothing, but bunch up my clothes and trip dripping into the living room.

To my relief, he doesn't come chasing me in hot pursuit like a Greek god after a naiad. He takes his time in the shower, even singing, building a stairway to paradise, again.

He emerges finally with a fog of steam, a towel tied at his hip, and he comes to me holding forth a lit cigarette.

"With my apologies, if I frightened you," says the prince.

I shake my head at the smoke. "It's getting late," I say. I have no idea what time it is, but this seems totally true nonetheless.

"Your nose is not bleeding. Maybe like hiccups, we scare it away." He grins, obviously pleased with his humor. "Kitty"—he tilts his wet head and smiles again at me—"don't be mad. It's nothing."

That, I know, is a lie, but I can't explain what the something is before he turns to recapture his wine glass from the table and strolls with it into the bedroom, from where he

calls, "Kitty, you are a lovely woman. Not so very young ...
Oldest in the class, eh?"

That stings. "Don't call me Kitty," I yell, but he doesn't
hear. He is dressing, I guess, humming something from
Carmen, and dancing around, by the sound of it, the
whooshes and clump landings of turns and jumps.

I put on my coat and hat. A new smell drifts in. Pot, clear
and sweet. I wonder. Have I now morphed by default into
Designated Driver? I wait by the door, and who is staring at
me from a photo on the wall but Tanaquil LeClercq. She is
dressed in a white tutu and tights and pointe shoes and is sitting slumped in a cloth-draped chair with her long legs lovely
but motionless before her. She looks as deeply sad as seems
humanly possible. I know the picture and that it was taken
after she got polio because Ursula hung a copy in her office
after her MS recurred. She told us about T.L. as a reminder to
savor each day, because you never know. You never know. The
picture shows what loss looks like, how sad and how beautiful. Unreal that the lovely librarian Nina would have this
photo too. Do all dancers have shrines to beauty and loss?

If Luis insists on driving, I can't argue. I don't have a
license, and I didn't bring my permit with me. And I don't
know where the hell to go, directionwise. But he is not
exactly the cheerful, capable, competent teacher I left with
this morning, eons ago.

He tries to postpone the trip. "It's snowing," he says as
he comes from Nina's bedroom. "Look out the window."

Snow.

5

THINGS GET FUZZY FROM HERE. LITERALLY. THE SNOW I SEE
spitting at the streetlights below Nina's apartment continues as
we slog across two quiet streets and along white sidewalks to
where the car sits like a frosted lump near the Academy. The
car's clock says only 3:00, but all the school windows are lit
and seem distant and lovely as a stage. Inside are the dancers;
outside, me, the poor little match girl looking in at the feast.

Luis says maybe we should spend the night since the
weather looks so bad, but I'm not dumb. Well, I am dumb
to say no let's go, but I have no choice.

No way could I stay with him. Right now, trying to
scrape snow and ice off the front window with my glove
and sleeve, I really, really, really want to be in my room,
warm with no one but Whisper.

He gets into the car and starts the engine and the
wipers, which swipe my arm. "Well, let's go," he says impa-
tiently. I can barely hear the muffled words.

I climb in. There could be a wall in the car between us,
or, more like, around him. A bubble, a box, an iron cage.
And I am partly glad. It occurs to me that he should be
caged. Gray streaks move outside my window as if the car is
being whipped by ghosts.

"Would the lights help?" I really don't know.

"Would the lights help?" he echoes in a squeaky, naggy
voice.

Oh man, this is ridiculous, but I don't want to die just 'cause his pride is hurt.

He pulls away from the curb too fast, spinning the tires and then lurching into the street. He skids through the *arrêt* sign at the corner and slides into a wide, fishtailing left turn. Luckily, no other cars get in our way on these skinny streets near the Academy, although now it occurs to me that it might be good to crash right here and let the police take care of Luis and the car while I run to the school for help. Everyone would understand. Even Nina would be nice. I could call home. They'd be in the barn. I'd leave a message. I'd have to stay at the school, in the dorm that I never got to see. That would be cool.

"Let's go back to the school," I say. "I … we can probably stay there."

"Oh, no," he says, "you want to go home. Fine. Home to Mama, home to Daddy and the cowies."

In spite of his nastiness his driving seems to improve through downtown, where streetlights have come on and traffic has increased. But he picks up speed again as he sails across the bridge, *bu-bunk, bu-bunk*, and out of the city. I want to quote *Bridges freeze before roads* from my driver's manual, but I don't. We skid around a sharp curve, skid through an underpass beneath a moving train. I don't know how he can see through the foggy window into the pelting snow. I wipe off the inside of the window as far as I can reach and fiddle with the controls for help defrosting the rest. There is before us—no joke—a billboard reading *Vous avez droit à deux erreurs. La Police.* You have a right to two mistakes. I wonder which exactly are mine and which are his.

When the road straightens out, he starts passing cars, trucks, whatever, clunking each time into the unplowed left lane and almost sliding onto the shoulder. I try closing my eyes; I try breathing deeply into my toes; I try gripping the door and holding my breath. The throbbing of my head returns and reaches my stomach and is climbing back up my throat.

"Can you slow down, please?" I say through my teeth as I try not to puke.

He puckers his mouth and leans forward, puffing out air in two spurts. The car goes faster, dashing around a big truck, grain or milk, crossing in front of it, bouncing onto the shoulder, and finally skidding to a stop.

"You drive," he says. He gets out of the car, opens the rear door, slides in, and sits, arms crossed, head back.

"I don't have a license," I say. The motor's running; the sleet is louder, faster, meaner; the wipers fan a wad of slush away every few seconds.

"Pfft! But I do. You have a permit. I know the rules. Drive."

He's fumbling in his pockets, with a bag, a pipe, a match. Dope.

I don't bother to remind him I didn't bring my permit. That he was pissed off by my lack of ID earlier in the day. I climb over the gully into the driver's seat. Slow and steady. How bad could it be? Slow and steady, Grampa style. *Never hurry, never worry.* He'd have long ago taken over the wheel or gotten out to walk.

The seat is warm from Luis and the heater and seems lower down to the floor. I scoot it forward and jerk the back more upright, turn on the headlights. He didn't have them on! I sit up straight, fasten my seat belt. I get the wipers going their fastest, turn up the defrost, and crank open the foggy side window to check for traffic. I ease onto the road.

Driving practically blind sucks, but it beats being a passenger. I fix on the flurry ahead and what little I can make out of the road. A sign reads "Max 70." Mph or kph? It doesn't matter. I go real slow, like about 20 mph, if that. I don't dare move my focus to check the speedometer, or even get good tunes on the radio. My CD player seems a stranger, far away in my bag, forgotten all the rotten day. I glance quickly into the mirror at Luis. He seems to be done with his treat and is dozing, head back, mouth open. Lovely. A car swooshes by, spraying slop on the window, and I panic for a second. This is not the time to be fretting about missing Aragorn. I invoke the spirit of bat-hood to guide me by sense beyond sight.

I am concentrating so hard to stay on the road that I have no energy to spare for confusion. I see and ignore signs, funny arrows pointing in curving directions like dance notation I've seen in Ursula's books. I pass little houses with cozy lights and barns lit up through the gray. Milking time.

It takes maybe two hours, but I finally see a sign, "VT

13 km," which I know, even in my glazed and fatigued state, means the car needs a licensed driver. I pull into one of the farm driveways that empty right onto the highway. The mailbox reads "Aube." If we get stuck at *une ferme*, I figure, they'll be nice people and we can talk *des vaches*. I can sleep flank to flank with the cowies and Luis can go to hell.

"Luis." I turn around and poke his knee. "Wake up." My thumb presses the seam of his black jeans, hard. I have very strong hands from starting each cow manually before milking, so this isn't exactly gentle, but hey, I am beat.

I tell him he has to drive through the border. I roll down the window to rouse him and air out the car. I don't know how savvy the guard's nose might be. Probably more savvy than mine.

He never says boo. I get out of the car and walk around, glad to breathe fresh, if frozen, air and stretch my legs. He gets out too, rubbing his face, and slumps into the driver's seat, then pushes it back with a grunt.

I consider climbing in the back to sleep but figure we both ought to look lively and unsuspicious for the *douanes*. Just two normal people, *professeur et étudiante*, driving home in a blinding blizzard with the windows open.

Luis still isn't talking but seems to summon the strength to perform well. How often he has told us he's a pro! He smooths down his hair, takes several swigs from my water bottle in the cup holder, without asking. He sloshes the water in his mouth and spits out through the open window. He turns on the radio and fiddles with static till

Piano Jazz theme music comes through. That I recognize because for some reason Mom switches it on every Friday night in the barn as we finish up. She doesn't sit with us on the bales, but she does switch to a lower gear sometimes.

Prepare to show identification. Declare all articles acquired outside the US. Luis slows at the customs booth, no line whatsoever, and a serious mustached man in a dark toque slides open his window. Luis silences the tunes.

The guard asks where we are going, how long we've been in Canada, are we American citizens, and if we bought anything. He asks for Luis's license, and I hand over my birth certificate, thanking Mom in my head. Luis, *naturellement,* to my relief and annoyance, is back in control. He is clear, not too effusive, and explains without overexplaining that I auditioned for a place at the dance academy, and was due home to help on the family farm. And that he has a new baby at home in Hope Springs, where he teaches at the college. Our families are expecting us; otherwise he would never be driving in these terrible conditions. He seems concerned but not overly so, and extremely competent. The consummate professional. Wow.

The guard hands back our papers and says, "The plows have been out, but go slow."

Luis drives on through. More snow, more silence.

The piano show comes back on with a tribute to Harold Arlan, the guy who wrote "Somewhere over the Rainbow." Who knew? I wonder if Luis did. I want to ask him if he likes *The Wizard of Oz* (I adore it), but there is nothing normal between us at this point, or maybe we've never had normal conversation.

His performance must have drained him because he doesn't look too good. He's white and squint-eyed, like *he* has the splitting headache now.

He snakes to a stop at the Welcome Center, where I pee and finally take out my contacts and put on my glasses, with relief. (Why did I ever care how I looked?) Funny how much better I am feeling—so good that after we return silent as ghosts from the restrooms, him with coffee, me with a fresh water bottle, I say, "I'll drive!" with such verve that he doesn't argue.

He shrugs, and helps brush the newest slop off the windshield. He gets in the passenger seat, not the back. I take that to signify he isn't so pissed anymore in either sense of the word, but maybe the front is just more comfortable. He sips while I get rolling, then reclines the seat, says, "Nice glasses," and lies back, eyes closed, out of it again. I notice he doesn't hook his seat belt, but he hasn't all day. Just that kind of guy.

I have to say, I am glad to be back in Vermont. Maybe if I lived right up here, way north, I'd feel differently, but it seems now after crossing the border that everything relaxes even as the daylight disappears; it feels less cramped, the road is smoother and better plowed. The familiar green signs with town names I recognize and food/gas signs in English—these comfort me.

I seriously want comfort. The car clock shows 7:25—it's

over twelve hours since we were here going in the opposite direction. But no clock can measure a day like this; it has been centuries since I left home, more than I can contemplate. I fix my attention on the road ahead, on my hands on the wheel at ten and two.

Dry snow is falling now, not sleet, and the wind has died. Even though it's totally dark I can see better and the road is well cleared.

It's peaceful with Luis asleep. Let sleeping dogs lie. A saying from Mom? No, Grampa again, when I used to pull on Waldo's ears.

I sure am getting my highway practice. I can write in "3–4 hours" in my log at home. Well, no. Mom would never sign it, since she will never know about this, since telling her would mean explaining why Luis, the adult experienced driver, wasn't driving in these conditions. I could just say I wanted the practice and he was willing, he trusted me. (Unlike *you*, I could imply.) But even to me this line of reasoning is bogus and seems outdated somehow. Could I even pretend I *wanted* to get my practice in a blinding snowstorm after a brutal day? She'd say, *What kind of person is he anyway, to let a kid drive? And where was Clara?* I don't want to get into that with her. Let sleeping dogs lie. I'll fill in the log later with legit hours driving Grampa G.W. and Roberta maybe to the Snowflake museum or to Kingdom Halls all over the state, or just do what Lacey and everyone else does and make up all the hours the night before the test. Whatever.

"Wuzzat?" Luis mutters without sitting up.

"Huh?" He's interrupting my thoughts.

"The siren."

I guess it's true—if you take away one sense, the others compensate. Luis, eyes closed, without any sense in some ways, hears the cop before I notice the flashing lights following us.

"God, Kit, slow down!"

Speeding? Me? I don't think so. I am so firmly in control. But now I'm not. The last thing I hear as I skid across the wake-up bumps, the shoulder, hit the guardrail hard, is Luis whooping like a loon.

6

BEFORE I OPEN MY EYES I KNOW I'M IN A HOSPITAL BY THE sheer quiet, the odd smell, the upright angle of my body. My head and right leg ache.

I remember what happened. I lie still with the worst possible truth. Luis is dead. I killed him. I've changed everything.

My mother's voice, a normal, inappropriate voice: "Kit, wake up now, you're fine."

She gives the facts. It's midnight. I have a concussion, a bruised sternum, and a badly sprained ankle. Luis broke his arm and bumped his knee. She holds on to my hand. Dad arrives at her side and says I was a damn fool to be driving in that crud. She shushes him.

Something has changed, but I have not changed everything. I'm dizzy with relief.

Next day, St. Patrick's Day, she takes me home. She has asked virtually no tricky questions including why Clara and Lola weren't in the car and why I was driving, or even how the audition went. It's all: can you stand on that foot, how's your head? First things first, I guess. "Last Rose of Summer" is playing on the truck radio, sung by an Irish tenor. Way sad. Is Mom the rose fading and I'm the mere bud, the tip of the bloom, opening, wary of opening? I don't think I like the song.

I seem to be super-sensitive to smells. The nurse

suggested a shower at the hospital, but I waited to take a bath at home. I reject my former favorite rose soap and use Dad's Irish Spring and wash my hair with Mom's stuff that smells of fake wild raspberries. They should make shampoo smelling of fresh hay. People who have been haying smell indescribably good. I remember my mother's hair after a late night unloading hay once when I was little. It swung into my face when she kissed me good night. I gathered it and held it over my face, sniffing deeply. I wanted to wrap myself in the smell. I told her I wanted a blanket of that good smell. You can sleep in the haymow, she said. No, your hair, your hay hair, Mommy, I want it. She pulled away laughing. I remember I made her happy that night about a million years ago.

She's very calm. She keeps saying I'm fine.

7

From my bed I hear Thunderbird greeting light with sound, a crow, a cry. He greets the day with enthusiasm and gets all the hens clucking. Quite the bandleader. Chaser of dourness. He keeps things moving. I hear Mom yelling, "Move over, buster, share the feast."

Mom loves those birds.

I used to call T-bird "Cock" just to tick off Mom. "How's Cock today? Want me to feed the chickens and Cock?"

Today, with a plastic bag over my air cast, I help her clean out the coop, heavy with winter's manure pack. I shovel, she ferries the wheelbarrow. With the snow and ice thawing we do good work. Then I limp along Jackrabbit Road just to test my ankle, and I see a flash of red fur dip behind the old schoolhouse foundation way up the road. I tell Dad about it. Says he wondered if there wasn't a den up there. He'll try to shoot the fox. Hates to, but the chickens come first.

8

SOME THINGS CHANGE. THE SEASONS CHANGE. SPRING
takes over. No more Ides of March snow. Warm drizzle for
this April Fool, then a week of mud, then bright sun like a
starting gun for our outdoor work. Fencing, more fencing,
spreading manure, plowing, planting corn, vaccinating,
hoof trimming, getting the heifers to pasture—Dad, Clay,
and Grampa are out straight. They hardly have time for the
cows, which Mom and I mostly milk, and we hire a new
guy to help with an experimental third milking. Dad thinks
this might be cheaper than a robot. His name, no kidding,
is Tim White, as close as I'll get to Timmy Snow, I know.

I find out you can milk just fine with a concussion and
a bruised sternum and a sprained ankle. You just go slow
and steady, Grampa style. I find that two-gallon freezer bags
are the best wrapping for my air cast, and I am extremely
careful not to step in manure.

When the vet comes I help vaccinate, I help move cows
for the hoof trimmer. I owe Dad for the hefty traffic ticket,
which surpassed my measly $150. But I love hooves anyway:
pretty as pointe shoes and more practical for walking.

Every day I wake early; when it isn't farm work I read
and write. I put together a portfolio for "assessment" with
papers on bats, on the Donner Party, on S.A.D. and MS,
on short stories (I compared "The Dead" and "The Yellow
Wallpaper"), on robotic milking systems versus three-times-

a-day milking. I prepare our farm account book for math work and for taxes due April 15. I reread my dance poem and "Oral History" but decide they are too personal to send. I remove them from my wall. I mean, why look back?

One afternoon Lacey drives over to visit, since I can't (and don't really want to) dance. She looks over my stuff and says that except for math my lame work isn't any lamer than the work of most tenth graders who actually go to school. She goes, "No exams. It must be cool to home-school." She also says I missed this amazing spoken-word guy who came in *and* the courtship of Ms. Bailey and Mr. Root, and prom is coming and by the way how is my ankle. She says she has started a bumper-sticker business. At least, that's what she's telling her mother to explain the money she gets selling "sunshine." She and Mike (Mike!) get beer and stuff from his older brother and leave it in this stump near The Hide where people leave their money.

About dance she says things are kind of falling apart. "I mean, no one blames you or anything, but without Luis teaching, things are dead. Clara gives these intense classes no one likes, endless barre combinations, pirouettes no one can do, too many beats. No one smiles. People are dropping out. Ursula has come back to help with the senior performance. And she uses a cane. You're lucky you're going away to school next year. You're going, right? You must have gotten in. Did you get in?"

She's obviously dying to know, but I don't tell Lacey much about That Day. I don't tell anyone anything except that the audition was fine, the weather sucked, I was driving because Luis was beat, I was going too fast, *mea culpa*. That's what everyone and their uncle knows. And that Luis broke his arm and hurt his knee in the crash, can't dance, isn't teaching.

Lacey says he limps, holds Lola in a cloth carrier, and cradles his arm in a sling as if he's got two babies. She never liked him.

I picture him as a rooster, one scaly leg drawn up, wings clipped. I tell her I'm still waiting to hear from the school. To be exact, I say, "Haven't heard a peep."

Four weeks after That Day, I come in late from the barn, tired, a little down, my head and chest aching. Nostalgically, I try to conjure Timmy. It would be his April vacation and we could be working with my E.D. 7, Janus, and Timmy's junior calf, Creemee, a lively dark Jersey, more correct than mine. I'd give him the best. He'd have gotten her to lead pretty well and I'd be so proud. I never wanted him getting spoiled, just hanging out with video games. Plus I like giving directions, coaching, bossing, whatever. But I have grown weary of that game. It takes too much energy, conjuring does; it isn't fun. I just trained my calf alone, matter-of-factly, being extra strict. I had no patience for her bouncing around. She's got a spot of ringworm that I treated with a paste of borage. Grammy showed me that ages ago. "Borage for courage," Grampa said when he saw what I was doing. He also patted my head, extra gently it seemed to me.

So, I just wash my hands and head to my room. But Mom calls from the kitchen. "Kit? Wait, wait. Don't disappear so soon. There's a phone message for you, and a letter. Ursula called. Call her, please," she says, "and look." She hands over an envelope, from Canada, smiling. I know she's trying to be nice. That's how she's been since the accident. But just then the letter seems like one of those dead rat gifts Whisper drags in and plops proudly on the kitchen floor.

Suddenly sick, that's how I feel. Canada to me means that dumb, dumb drive, the accident, Luis and the *Psycho* scene. So far it's been easy to avoid him, easier than it was in the car when *his* unbelted elbow gave me the damn concussion. I can't dance, so I don't run into him. He hasn't called, hasn't asked how I'm doing. I'm sorry he broke his other arm and bruised a knee, all of which seriously stinks for a dancer. But I'm doing my utmost by not telling anyone it serves him right. Just deserts and all that.

I figure my ankle is similar punishment. Both of us sidelined: me to the barn, him to his baby.

I sincerely hope he won't be able to dance till Lola can walk.

Their stint at Hope Springs is almost up anyway. After the student show the holy family will be moving on. I just stay away. It's not like I don't have plenty to do.

Besides, every day I spend an hour in my "studio" above the milk house, stretching and stuff. It's enough. Dad saw me there one night when he was getting hay. He peeked in at me after chores and said, "As soon as things slow down a bit, me and Clay and Tim will clean this crap outta here and make it nice, okay?" I told him great. Whatever. I told him no hurry.

So as I take the letter I'm wondering why Ursula would want to talk to me now. She came to the hospital when I was sleeping, brought flowers, told Mom she was trying to be less a regular there herself and hoped I'd go home soon. Was she well enough to sniff a rat? And would the rat be Luis or me?

I take the letter and the phone to my room. I rip open the letter and skim. *Dear Katherine ... Impressed with your musicality ... We see great talent and potential ... However, we regret ...*

I didn't get in. Something about under-accomplishment for my age, especially in pointe work but also in clarity of line. I toss the letter on the floor. I call Ursula.

When I hear her voice I say, "It's Kit," and start to cry. I mean weep—big, wet, gasping, throat-clutching sobs.

"What, Kit?" she says. "Did you get the letter? What's wrong? Is this for the letter?"

It's not. But I can't say it: that I hadn't heard her voice in so long. It's music I've missed. I've missed my teacher.

"But Kit, it's wonderful news. It's better this way. Four whole weeks and a full scholarship! Congratulations!"

I don't know what she's talking about, of course, because I haven't finished the ratty letter. I murmur, "What?"

She says, "Read it."

I fish it off my friend the floor, and this time I read that on the basis of "talent and potential," Mr. L. is offering me their residential summer program in July, four weeks of daily ballet as well as modern, jazz, character, and choreography, *gratuitement*.

"Kit," Ursula is asking, "are you there?"

I am thinking: about the nice piano lady and the long, lighted windows, about the library with the tall shelves and Degas prints on the walls, about living in a building with a carpeted gyroscopic stairway and chandeliers. And about walking on the pavement, *sans* snow, in July. July? I'll miss the fair and showing E.D. 7, and I'll miss some of the haying. Probably not enough of the haying.

"But my ankle," I say. "I haven't been dancing."

She wants to see it, and insists that I meet her at the studio tomorrow. She has already asked Cyn to drive me. She wants to see her too. Cyn, she calls her. When did they get so chummy?

I lie in bed that night wondering if she wants to discuss not only my ankle but also Luis. I wonder if somehow she knows, like a spirit, things unseen. Does my mother know? Are they planning to gang up on me about it? I wonder too as I have before if the dead can see us living. Did Grammy see me that day, in the shower? The thought is unbearable.

Before That Day, everything was blurry and exciting. His attention in and out of class made me feel special, like an artist. My dancing improved. I felt my body becoming a playable instrument, capable of beauty.

Now I see one thing clear. I needed Luis that day to be my teacher, and he wasn't. He was like Thunderbird, mindlessly strutting. But it wasn't all his fault. Hadn't I imagined his touch the way he touched me? I just thought he'd be nicer. I mean, if Luis had been *nicer* I might have done anything. I wasn't thinking, *Oh he's married, oh Clara, oh Lola.* I mean, I don't know if I ran out of the shower because it was wrong or because he smelled like sour wine and hadn't liked my audition or because I just freaked. How could I be so dumb? How could he be so mean?

So, anyway, I don't want to talk about it because I don't exactly blame him and I don't exactly blame me and I don't want any more trouble.

9

THE NEXT MORNING AFTER ARRIVING AT THE COLLEGE
I can't figure out why Mom brought along the cane we keep
in the barn for herding cows, since my ankle isn't *that* bad,
but then I see Ursula walking toward us. She lists to the
right as if dizzy. She wraps me in her arms and then hugs
my mother, takes the cane, and says, "You remembered.
This is less crone-ish than the one the doctor gave me."

While we sit in her office and talk, she fans herself
with a new fan like one Mom had that I used to play dress-
up with. It *is* Mom's fan. I'm disoriented.

We don't talk about Luis. We talk about me, and the
summer program, and what could happen after that, dance-
wise. Ursula gently checks out my ankle and gives me some
exercises. She says she is feeling better and is expecting
remission. She is relying upon Dr. Will Power and Dr. Take
Care of Yourself and some excellent medicine. She will not
however be able to give the dance program and me (in par-
ticular, she says) the energy we need and deserve. I start to
cry. I don't think I'm so special. She takes my hand. Luis
and Clara, as I might have heard, can't stay. She looks at me
when she says this and waits a beat. And another. I shrug
and wipe my eyes.

"Don't cry for them. It wasn't a great match," she says.
That is the end of that.

But, she says, she has a friend, an incredible dancer

and teacher, currently in Hanover; she'll come for a year. Ursula says she is "brilliant" and perfect for me, and greater than the Hope Springs College dance program deserves. "She is doing this as a favor. Being sick is showing me how kind people are." Her eyes glisten, but she smiles. "Of course when she sees you in class, and Eva"—that's one of the twelve-year-olds—"and Henry, she'll be thrilled."

My mother sits on the edge of her chair just listening, very quiet.

"Will you two watch something?" Ursula asks. "I'm teaching this dance to Naheema for the senior performance, but I want to do it for you. It really calls for an older dancer."

She gets up slowly, and we follow her into the studio. It smells of wax and roses and now of our perfume of hay and iodine.

It's the oddest thing: me and Mom sitting on the floor together in the front of the studio where I sat to watch for the first time years ago on a cleaning day. My leg stretches out to the side with the air cast looking really long. Mom sits cross-legged like a skinny white-haired kid in jeans honestly destroyed at the knees.

Ursula presents us with a dance by Isadora Duncan called "Mother." It is clear, direct, like an arrow to the heart. Ursula in her usual costume, her long black skirt and black leotard, travels on a diagonal, upstage left to down right, taking three steps with her hand behind her guiding a small child. I see the child. She draws the child forward and the child draws her back, again. She pulls like a draft horse. She is a beast of burden. She lifts her eyes and then her arm to the future; she turns back to the child. She cradles the child. She pulls him close. She turns him to us *en face*; Ursula shows him us, the world, out, out beyond where Mom and I sit. On one knee now, she pushes the child away, watches, follows with her eyes and heart, oh, sees him returning, and catches him in her arms, almost falling over. (Mom gasps. I look at her, her arm across her own chest; I can't watch her.) Ursula embraces the child again and it turns into a tiny baby in her arms and then as she pulls the baby to her heart it vanishes and her hands slide down her breasts, her belly, to the floor. The mother looks to her hands, the floor, then out to the diagonal again, hears hope in the music, a solo piano of course, looks out, sees something, ah, the child? and raises her arm like a flag, smiles, and folds softly into the floor.

That's the story, but the majesty is in Ursula's measured steps, held steady only by the music.

My eyes fill again. When I turn to Mom her cheeks are wet. We laugh. She reaches to my face and brushes a tear before it touches my mouth. Somehow she doesn't look S.A.D.

On the way home it seems easy to ask, "Did that make you think of Timmy?"

"Timmy?" she says with a fragile smile. "More of you and me, and of Grammy too. Did I ever tell you that before she died her hand gave this little wave?" Mom took her right hand off the wheel, moved it side to side, a little fan. Mom smiles.

"No, you didn't tell me." But I'm thinking that's good, Mom waving.

"Only, I don't think the mother in that dance dies at the end." Mom is discussing Art. I am amazed. "She's just resting. Whew! Kid grown, job done."

"Hmm." I don't know what else to say.

At the senior show I see Naheema perform "Mother" differently, more grace, less power. I sit on the aisle, where my air cast can stretch. Mom can't be there because the whitewasher comes to do the barn tomorrow and she has to brush down cobwebs. She promised to spare what spiders she can, knowing I like them almost as much as bats. I feel her in the blank space by my side. Luckily Lacey sits on my other side and luckily she has the sense to go, "Umm, wow," at the end. Luis sits way up front and we leave before he does. At the door Thaddeus rushes up and scoops me up in a hug. "Good job!" he says.

I write to Ursula to thank her for the dance and she answers by coming to the farm bringing CDs: the Scriabin piano music from "Mother," more Chopin, and several of ballet-class music for me to use on my own while I heal. I ask if maybe she thinks the Academy gives piano lessons. She says, "I imagine so." Maybe I'll take some when I'm there. I'm ready for something new.

I figure, at the Academy, they can call me Katherine.

French pronunciation doesn't sound the "th," so I'll hear the "Kat" part and think of Whisper at home.

In the fall, who knows? Maybe back to high school. Mom has already asked if I'd like that. I asked if she was tired of running a school. "I'm a farmer, Kit," she said, frowning. "I'm sorry, I haven't been much of a teacher."

"Hey hey hey," I said, play-punching her arm, "you were fine. I've seen worse." This much I know: in the Snow "No School" I learned how to learn stuff and avoid creeps. More or less.

In the future, *on verra*. I'm trying not to conjure what I want because I really don't know. Maybe I'll get into the Academy for my senior year or maybe Ursula will be back teaching at Hope Springs. Lacey says I should study dance therapy in college because, of all the nutcases she knows, I have the best moves. She says when she's undecided about stuff her mother tells her to do Child's Pose, this yoga bow on knees, to the floor. Lay yourself at the feet of the universe, her mother says, and everything will work out. Lacey is trying to figure how to put that philosophy on a bumper sticker.

Turns out Grampa G.W. can't bring himself to actually join the J.W.'s, despite his affection for Roberta, because he wants a less energetic religion, one without homework. Figures he's done his homework. Says he might sign on to one of those religions where sitting or breathing is the activity, or smoking a pipe maybe, drinking a drink. Besides, he says he cannot divest himself of the Mary statue in Grammy's garden. "She's quite a gal once you get to know her." He sits in the rickety folding chair he pulled from our last year's lawn sale, listens to the birds, talks to his Rosemary, talks to the statue. Grammy Rose must love it. He didn't want the statue much to begin with, but Grammy saw it at a junkyard up near North Bay once when they went fishing with her brother in Canada. She always liked Mary.

Good morning sweet Jesus my savior, Good morning sweet Mary my mother, I give you my heart, my soul, and my life. Keep me from sin this day and forever. Every day at waking. Then they got up together, him to the barn, her to the kitchen, her garden, her daughter, her job at school. Every day.

Mom and I have taken on weeding the herbs, slowly finding what all Grammy had in there. Grampa mutters while we weed, "Two can accomplish more than twice as much as one. If one falls, the other pulls him up, but if a man falls when he is alone, he is in trouble." It's a quote from Ecclesiastes, he says, but is he referring to weeding, or what?

I think of partnering in the dancing sense and, ouch, how it didn't work out for me. Yet. Yet. There's hope. I mean, here's me and Mom, an unlikely duet, at truce.

Even Grammy and Grampa, I bet it wasn't so sweet every day, but maybe. It was a while ago. Grammy's been dead for over a year and a half, but maybe not to Grampa. Here he is in the herb garden, him and Waldo, under the outspread hands of Our Lady. His other ladies on their knees among herbs and weeds. Abundance is the only word for this healing collection. I aim to dry what we can find this year and replenish the jars in the trailer cupboard. Then Mom and Grampa G.W. will tell me what they remember of how to use the herbs. What they don't remember, I'll find out somehow. I remember Grammy quoting the dowser's motto: *Indago felix, the fruitful search.* It means you find things as you need them. I've already discovered for Ursula that teas of catnip and chamomile supposedly help MS. There are always books, and, like air, sources of info everywhere.

The summer Grammy was dying Mom named all the calves after herbs: Lavender, Borage, Peppermint, Thyme, Chamomile, Burdock, Comfrey, Nettle, Dandelion, Periwinkle, Chicory, Angelica, Purslane, and of course Rosemary. They're all grown now, and due to calve this summer and fall. I'll miss a few of the births, but not most. That's something else to look forward to. The calves'll be incredibly cute but will need a lot of care. I'll help when I can.